"I do know that you should l[ove?] family. Love them, keep them safe, whatever they do."

And there it was. Right there. The reason he needed to step away. If he hadn't recognized her vulnerability within minutes of setting eyes on her, her belief in the importance of family and all the things he despised would have sent up the kind of warning flares that a man who believed in nothing and no one would do well to heed.

Take your hands off her now, McElroy.

Let her go…

His legs had ignored him. His hands were still resting just below her shoulder blades, keeping her close, his thighs against her hips, and this time he'd didn't waste time asking himself whether he should kiss her.

He had to know.

Her eyes widened slightly as his mouth slowly descended, giving her all the time in the world to say no, to do what he was unable to do and step back.

Her lips did part, as if she might say something, but all that emerged was a little quiver of breath, warm, faintly chocolately, mingling with his own, fizzing through his blood, intoxicating as vintage champagne. He was within a hair's breadth of going to hell in a handcart when a crunch on the gravel, and a loud, "It's still here!' warned them that they were no longer alone.

LIZ FIELDING

Tempted by Trouble

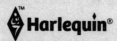

Harlequin®

TORONTO NEW YORK LONDON
AMSTERDAM PARIS SYDNEY HAMBURG
STOCKHOLM ATHENS TOKYO MILAN MADRID
PRAGUE WARSAW BUDAPEST AUCKLAND

Recycling programs
for this product may
not exist in your area.

ISBN-13: 978-0-373-17736-3

TEMPTED BY TROUBLE

First North American Publication 2011

Copyright © 2011 by Liz Fielding

This edition published by arrangement with Harlequin Books S.A.

For questions and comments about the quality of this book please contact us at Customer_eCare@Harlequin.ca.

® and TM are trademarks of the publisher. Trademarks indicated with ® are registered in the United States Patent and Trademark Office, the Canadian Trade Marks Office and in other countries.

www.Harlequin.com

Printed in U.S.A.

Liz Fielding was born with itchy feet. She made it to Zambia before her twenty-first birthday and, gathering her own special hero and a couple of children on the way, lived in Botswana, Kenya and Bahrain—with pauses for sightseeing pretty much everywhere in between.

She finally came to a full stop in a tiny Welsh village cradled by misty hills, and these days—mostly—leaves her pen to do the traveling.

When she's not sorting out the lives and loves of her characters, she potters in the garden, reads her favorite authors and spends a lot of time wondering, *What if*....

For news of upcoming books—and to sign up for her occasional newsletter—visit Liz's website at www.lizfielding.com.

CHAPTER ONE

Life is like ice cream: you have to take it one lick at a time.

—Rosie's Diary

'LOVAGE AMERY?'

If ever there had been a moment to follow Gran's example and check her reflection in the mirror before she opened the front door, Elle decided, this was it.

On her knees and up to her rubber gloves in soapy water when the doorbell rang, she hadn't bothered to stop and fix hair sliding out of its elastic band. And there wasn't much she could have done about a face pink and shiny from a day spent catching up with the housework while everyone was out, culminating in scrubbing the kitchen floor.

It was the complete Cinderella workout.

She couldn't afford a fancy gym membership and, as she was always telling her sisters, cleaning was a lot more productive than pounding a treadmill. Not that they'd ever been sufficiently impressed by the argument to join in.

Lucky them.

Even sweaty Lycra had to be a better look than an ancient shirt tied around the waist with an equally geriatric psychedelic tie. Sexier than the jeans bagging damply around her knees.

It wouldn't normally have bothered her and, to be fair, the man standing on the doorstep hadn't made much of an effort, either. His thick dark hair was sticking up in a just-got-out-of-bed look and his chin was darkened with what might be designer stubble but was more likely to be a disinclination to shave on Saturday, when he didn't have to go into the office.

Always assuming that he had an office to go to. Or a job.

Like her, he was wearing ancient jeans, in his case topped with a T-shirt that should have been banished to the duster box. The difference was that on him it looked mouth-wateringly good. So good that she barely noticed that he'd made free with a name she'd been trying to keep to herself since she'd started kindergarten.

Swiftly peeling off the yellow rubber gloves she'd kept on as a 'Sorry, can't stop' defence against one of the neighbours dropping by with some excuse to have a nose around, entertain the post office queue with insider gossip on just how bad things were at Gable End, she tossed them carelessly over her shoulder.

'Who wants to know?' she asked.

Her hormones might be ready to throw caution to the wind—they were Amery hormones, after all—but while they might have escaped into the yard for a little exercise, she wasn't about to let them go 'walkies'.

'Sean McElroy.'

His voice matched the looks. Low, sexy, soft as Irish mist. And her hormones flung themselves at the gate like a half-grown puppy in a let-me-at-him response as he offered his hand.

Cool, a little rough, reassuringly large, it swallowed hers up as she took it without thinking, said, 'How d'you do?' in a voice perilously close to the one her grandmother used when she met a good-looking man. With that hint of breathiness that spelled trouble.

'I'm doing just fine,' he replied, his slow smile obliterating all memory of the way she looked. Her hair, the lack of make-up and damp knees. It made crinkles around those mesmerisingly blue eyes and they fanned out comfortably in a way that suggested they felt right at home there.

Elle had begun to believe that she'd bypassed the gene that reduced all Amery women to putty in the presence of a good looking man.

Caught off guard, she discovered that she'd been fooling herself.

The only reason she'd escaped so far, it seemed, was because until this moment she hadn't met a man with eyes of that particularly intense shade of blue.

A man with shoulders wide enough to carry the troubles of the world and tall enough not to make her feel awkward about her height, which had been giving her a hard time since she'd hit a growth spurt somewhere around her twelfth birthday. With a voice that seemed to whisper right through her bones until it reached her toes.

Even now they were curling inside her old trainers in pure ecstasy.

He epitomised the casual, devil-may-care, bad-boy look of the travelling men who, for centuries, had arrived on the village common in the first week of June with the annual fair and departed a few days later, leaving a trail of broken hearts and the occasional fatherless baby in their wake.

Trouble.

But, riveted to the spot, her hand still in his, all it needed was for fairground waltzer music to start up in the background and she'd have been twirling away on a fluffy pink cloud without a thought in her head.

The realisation was enough to bring her crashing back to her senses and, finally letting go of his hand, she took half a step back.

'What do you want, Mr McElroy?'

His eyebrows lifted a fraction at the swift change from drooling welcome to defensive aggression.

'Not a what, a who. I have a delivery for Lovage Amery.'

Oh, no…

Back to earth with a bump.

She hadn't ordered anything—she couldn't afford anything that would require delivery—but she had a grandmother who lived in a fantasy world. And her name was Lovage, too.

But all the questions tumbling out of her brain—the what, the who, the 'how much?' stuff—hit a traffic jam as his smile widened, reaching the parts of her that ordinary smiles couldn't touch.

Her pulse, her knees, some point just below her midriff that was slowly dissolving to jelly.

'If you'll just take this…'

She looked down and discovered that this delectable, sinewy package that had those drooling hormones sitting up and begging for whatever trouble he had in mind was offering her a large brown envelope.

The last time one of those had come calling for 'Lovage Amery' she'd taken it without a concern in the world, smiling right back at the man offering it to her.

She'd been younger then. About to start college, embark on her future, unaware that life had yet one more sucker punch to throw at her.

'What is it?' she asked, regretting the abandonment of the rubber gloves. Regretting answering the door.

'Rosie,' he said. As if that explained everything. 'You are expecting her?'

She must have looked as blank as she felt because he half turned and with a careless wave of the envelope, gestured towards the side of the house.

She leaned forward just far enough to see the front of a large pink and white van that had been backed up towards the garage.

She stared at it, expecting to see some disreputable dog sticking its head out of the window. She'd banned her sister from bringing home any more strays from the rescue shelter. The last one had broken not only their hearts, but what remained of their bank balance. But Geli was not above getting someone else to do her dirty work.

'Where is she?' she asked. Then, realising this practically constituted an acceptance, 'No. Whatever Geli said, I can't possibly take another dog. The vet's bills for the last one—'

'Rosie isn't a dog,' he said, and now he was the one looking confused. 'That's Rosie.'

She frowned, stared at the picture of an ice cream sundae on the van door, little cones on the roof, and suddenly realised what she was looking at.

'Rosie is an ice cream van?'

'Congratulations.'

Elle frowned. Congratulations? Had she won it in one of the many competitions she'd entered in a fit of post-Christmas despair when the washing machine had sprung a leak on the same day as the electricity bill had arrived?

Surely not.

She hadn't had any warning of its arrival. No phone call. No letter informing her of her good fortune. Which was understandable.

This would have to be the booby prize because, desperate as she was, she wouldn't have entered a competition offering a second-hand ice cream van as first prize.

She wouldn't have entered one offering a *new* ice cream van, but at least she could have sold it and bought a new washing machine, one with a low energy programme—thus dealing with two problems at once—with the proceeds.

While unfamiliar with the latest trends in transport, even she could see that Rosie's lines were distinctly last century.

Already the sorry owner of an ancient car that had failed its annual MOT test with a list of faults a mile long, the last thing she needed was to be lumbered with more scrap.

'Congratulations?' she repeated.

'You appear to have twenty-twenty vision,' he teased.

'A very *old* ice cream van,' she pointed out, doing her best to ignore the gotcha grin, the faded black T-shirt clinging to those enticing shoulders and figure out what the heck was going on.

'Actually, she's a nineteen sixty-two Commer ice cream van in her original livery,' he said, without a hint of apology. On the contrary, he seemed to be under the impression that it was a good thing.

'Nineteen sixty-two!'

It beat the wreck in the garage, which had rolled off the assembly line when she was still in primary school, by thirty years. That was a stripling youth compared to Rosie, which had taken to the road when her grandmother was still in school.

'The old girl's vintage,' Sean confirmed. 'She's your Great-Uncle Basil's pride and joy, but right now she's in need of a good home.'

As he said this, he looked over her shoulder into the house, no doubt intending to emphasize the point.

He didn't visibly flinch but the hall, like the rest of the house, was desperately in need of a coat of paint. It was also piled up with discarded shoes, coats and all the other stuff that teenagers seemed to think belonged on the floor. And of course, her rubber gloves.

That was the bad news.

The good news was that he couldn't see where the carpet had been chewed by the dog that had caused them all so much grief.

'Vintage,' she repeated sharply, forcing him to look at her instead of the mess behind her. 'Well, it would certainly fit right in around here. There's just one small problem.'

More than one if she was being honest and honestly, despite the fact that the aged family car had failed its annual test and she was desperate for some transport, she wasn't prepared to take possession of a vehicle that was short on seats and heavy on fuel.

Walking, as she was always telling her sisters, was good for you. Shaped up the legs. Pumped blood around the body and made the brain work harder. And they all had a duty to the planet to walk more. Or use public transport.

She walked. They used public transport.

There was absolutely no chance that either of her sisters would consider using the bike when it meant wearing an unflattering helmet and looking, in their words, 'like a dork' when they arrived at school and college, respectively.

'Which is?' he prompted.

She didn't bother him with the financial downside of her situation, but kept it simple.

'I don't have a Great Uncle Basil.'

Finally a frown. It didn't lessen the attraction, just made him look thoughtful, studious. Even more hormone-twangingly desirable.

'You *are* Lovage Amery?' he asked, catching up with the fact that, while she hadn't denied it, she hadn't confirmed it either. 'And this *is* Gable End, The Common, Longbourne.'

She was slow to confirm it and, twigging to her reluctance to own up to the name, the address, he glanced back at the wide wooden gate propped wide open and immovable for as long as she could remember. The letters that spelled out the words 'Gable End' were faded almost to nothing, but denial was pointless.

'Obviously there has been some kind of mistake,' she said with all the conviction she could muster. Maybe. Her grandmother might well know someone named Basil who needed somewhere to park his ice cream van, but he wasn't her uncle, great or otherwise. And, even if she'd wanted to—and she didn't—she had no time to take on an ice cream round. End of, as Geli was so fond of saying. 'Please take it away.'

'I will.' Her relieved smile was a fraction too fast. 'If you'll just help me get to the bottom of this.'

'Some kind of muddle in the paperwork?' she offered. 'Take it up with Basil.'

'It's not a common name. Lovage,' he said, ignoring her excellent advice.

'There's a good reason for that,' she muttered.

One of his eyebrows kicked up and something in her midriff imitated the action. Without thinking, Elle found herself checking his left hand for a wedding band. It was bare, but that didn't mean a thing. No man that good-looking could possibly be unattached. And, even if he was, she reminded herself, she wasn't. Very firmly attached to a whole heap of responsibilities.

Two sisters still in full-time education, a grandmother who lived in her own make-believe world, and a house that sucked up every spare penny she earned working shifts in a dead-end job so that she could fit around them all.

'You don't like it?' he asked.

'No… Yes…' It wasn't that she didn't like her name. 'Sadly, it tends to rouse the infantile in the male, no matter how old they are.'

'Men can be their own worst enemies,' he admitted. Then said it again. 'Lovage…'

This time he lingered over the name, testing it, giving it a deliciously soft lilt, making it sound very grown-up. And she discovered he didn't need the smile to turn her bones to putty.

She reached for the door, needing something to hang on to.

'Are you okay?' he asked.

'Fine,' she snapped, telling herself to get a grip.

The man was trying to lumber her with a superannuated piece of junk. Or, worse, was a con artist distracting her while an accomplice—maybe Basil himself—slipped around the back of the house and made off with anything not nailed down. Well, good luck with that one. But, whatever he was up to, it was a cast-iron certainty that flirting was something that came to him as naturally as breathing. And she was being sucked in.

'If that's all?' she enquired.

'No, wait!'

She hesitated a second too long.

'Right name. Tick. Right address. Tick—'

'Annoying male, tick,' she flashed back at him, determined to put an end to this. Whatever *this* was.

'You may well be right,' he agreed, amused rather than annoyed. Which was annoying. 'But, while you might not know your Great-Uncle Basil, I think you're going to have to accept that he knows you.' He looked down at the envelope he was holding, then up at her. 'Tell me, are you all named after herbs in your family?'

She opened her mouth, then, deciding not to go there, said, 'Tell me, Mr McElroy, does she…it,' she corrected herself, refusing to fall into the trap of thinking of the van as anything other than an inanimate object 'does it go?'

'I drove her here,' he pointed out, the smile enticing, mouth-wateringly sexy. Confident that he'd got her. 'I'll take you for a spin in her so that I can talk you through her little eccentricities, if you like,' he went on before she could complete her punchline, tell him to start it up and drive it away. 'She's a lovely old girl, but she has her moods.'

'Oh, right. You're telling me she's a *cranky* old ice cream van.'

'That's a bit harsh.' He leaned his shoulder against the door frame, totally relaxed, oblivious of the fact that the rose scrambling over the porch had dropped pink petals over his thick dark hair and on one of those broad shoulders. 'Shall we say she's an old ice cream van with bags of character?'

'Let's not,' she replied, doing her best to get a grip of her tongue, her hormones, her senses, all of which were urging her to forget her problems, throw caution to the wind and, for once in her life, say yes instead of no. 'I'm sorry, Mr McElroy—'

'Sean—'

'I'm sorry, *Mr McElroy*,' she reiterated, refusing to be sidetracked, 'but my mother told me never to take a ride with a stranger.'

A classic case of do as I say rather than do as I do, obviously. In similar circumstances, her mother wouldn't have hesitated.

She'd have grabbed the adventure and, jingle blaring, driven around the village scandalising the neighbours.

But, gorgeous though Sean McElroy undoubtedly was, she wasn't about to make the same mistakes as her mother. And while he was still trying to get his head around the fact that she'd turned him down flat, she took a full step back and shut the door. Then she slipped the security chain into place, although whether it was to keep him out or herself in she couldn't have said.

He didn't move. His shadow was still clearly visible behind one of the stained glass panels that flanked the door and, realising that he might be able to see her pinned to the spot, her heart racing, she grabbed the rubber gloves and beat a hasty retreat to the safety of the kitchen.

Today was rapidly turning into a double scrub day and, back on her knees, she went at it with even more vigour, her pulse pounding in her ears as she waited for the bell to ring again.

It didn't.

Regret warred with relief. It was a gorgeous May day and the thought of a spin in an ice cream van with a good-looking man called to everything young and frivolous locked up inside her. Everything she had never been. Even the scent of the lilac, wafting in through the kitchen door, seemed hell-bent on enticing her to abandon her responsibilities for an hour and have some fun.

She shook her head. Dangerous stuff, fun, and she attacked the floor with the brush, scrubbing at the already spotless quarry tiles, taking her frustration out on something inanimate while she tried to forget Sean McElroy's blue eyes and concentrate on today's problem. How to conjure two hundred and fifty pounds out of thin air to pay for Geli's school trip to France.

There was nothing for it. She was going to have to bite the bullet and ask her boss for an extra shift.

Sean caught his breath.

He'd been having trouble with it ever since the door of Gable

End had been thrown open to reveal Lovage Amery, cheeks flushed, dark hair escaping the elastic band struggling—and failing—to hold it out of a pair of huge hazel eyes.

Being a step up, she'd been on a level with him, which meant that her full, soft lips, a luscious figure oozing sex appeal, had been right in his face.

That she was totally oblivious of the effect created by all that unrestrained womanhood made it all the more enticing. All the more dangerous.

Furious as he was with Basil, he'd enjoyed the unexpected encounter and, while he was not fool enough to imagine he was irresistible, he thought that she'd been enjoying it, too. She'd certainly been giving as good as she got.

It was a long time since a woman had hit all the right buttons with quite that force and she hadn't even been trying.

Maybe that was part of the attraction.

He'd caught her unawares and, unlike most women of his acquaintance, she hadn't been wearing a mask, showing him what she thought he'd want to see.

Part of the attraction, all of the danger.

He'd as good as forgotten why he was there and the suddenness of her move had taken him by surprise. He couldn't remember the last time he'd been despatched quite so summarily by a woman but the rattle of the security chain going up had a finality about it that suggested ringing the doorbell again would be a waste of time.

He looked at the envelope Basil Amery had pushed through his door while he was in London, along with a note asking him to deliver it and Rosie to Lovage Amery.

He'd been furious. As if he didn't have better things to do, but it was typical of the man to take advantage. Typical of him to disappear without explanation.

True, his irritation had evaporated when the door had opened but, while it was tempting to take advantage of the side gate, standing wide open, and follow up his encounter with the luscious Miss Amery, on this occasion he decided that discretion was the better part of valour.

It would take more than a pair of pretty eyes to draw him into the centre of someone else's family drama. He had enough of that in his own backyard.

A pity, but he'd delivered Rosie. Job done.

CHAPTER TWO

Take plenty of exercise. Always run after the ice cream van.

—Rosie's Diary

ELLE, hot, flustered and decidedly bothered from her encounter with Sean McElroy, found her concentration slipping, her ears straining to hear the van start up, the crunch of tyres on gravel as it drove away.

It was all nonsense, she told herself, mopping up the suds, sitting back on her heels. She'd never heard of anyone called Basil Amery. It had to be a mistake. But the silence bothered her. While she hadn't heard the van arrive, she hadn't been listening. She had, however, been listening for it to leave.

The sudden rattle of the letter box made her jump. That was the only reason her heart was pounding, she told herself as she leapt to her feet. She wasn't in the habit of racing to pick up the post—it rarely contained anything but bills and she could wait for those—but it was an excuse to check that he'd gone.

There were two things on the mat. The brown envelope Sean McElroy had been holding and a bunch of keys. He couldn't, she told herself. He wouldn't... But the key fob was an ice cream cornet and she flung open the door.

Rosie was still sitting on the drive, exactly where he'd parked her.

'Sean McElroy!' she called, half expecting him to be

sitting in the van, grinning at having tricked her into opening the door.

He wasn't and, in a sudden panic, she ran to the gate, looking up and down the lane. Unless he'd had someone follow him in a car, he'd have to walk, or catch a bus.

She spun around, desperately checking the somewhat wild shrubbery.

Nothing. She was, apparently, quite wrong.

He could.

He had.

Abandoned Rosie on her doorstep.

'If you're looking for the van driver, Elle, he rode off in that direction.'

Elle inwardly groaned. Mrs Fisher, her next door neighbour, was bright-eyed with excitement as she stepped up to take a closer look at Rosie.

'Rode?'

'He had one of those fold-up bikes. Are you taking on an ice cream round?' she asked.

The internal groan reached a crescendo. The village gossips considered the Amery family their own private soap opera and whatever she said would be chewed over at length in the village shop.

'Sorry, Mrs Fisher, I can hear my phone,' she said, legging it inside, pushing the door shut behind her. If she'd left it open the woman would have considered it an invitation to walk in.

She sat on the bottom of the stairs holding the envelope, staring at the name and address which was, without doubt, hers.

Then she tore it open and tipped out the contents. A dark pink notebook with 'Bookings' written on the cover. A bells and whistles cellphone, the kind that would have her sisters drooling. There were a couple of official-looking printed sheets of paper. One was the logbook for the van, which told her that it was registered to Basil Amery of Keeper's Cottage, Haughton Manor, the other was an insurance certificate.

There was also a cream envelope.

She turned it over. There was nothing written on it, no name or address, but that had been on the brown envelope. She put her thumb beneath the flap and took out the single sheet of matching paper inside. Unfolded it.

Dear Lally, it began, and her heart sank as she read her grandmother's pet name.

Remember how you found me, all those years ago? Sitting by the village pond, confused, afraid, ready to end it all?

You saved me that day, my life, my sanity, and what happened afterwards wasn't your fault. Not Bernard's either. My brother and I were chalk and cheese but we are as we're made and there's nothing that can change us. Maybe, if our mother had still been alive, things would have been different, but there's no point in dwelling on it. The past is past.

I've kept my promise and stayed away from the family. I caused enough heartache and you and Lavender's girls have had more than enough of that to bear, losing Bernard and Lavender, without me turning up to dredge up the past, old scandals. The truth, however, is that I'm getting old and home called. Last year I took a cottage on the Haughton Manor estate and I've been working up the courage to write to you, but courage was never my strong point and now I've left it too late.

I have met your lovely granddaughter, though. I had lunch at the Blue Boar a couple of months ago and she served me. She was so like you, Lally—all your charm, your pretty smile—that I asked someone who she was. She even has your name. And here, I'm afraid, comes the crunch. You knew there would be a crunch, didn't you?

Rosie, who by now you'll have met, is a little hobby of mine. I do the occasional party, public event, you know the kind of thing, just to cover the costs of keeping her.

The occasional charity do for my soul. Unfortunately, events have rather overtaken me and I have to go away for a while but there are people I've made promises to, people I can't let down and I thought perhaps you and your granddaughter might take it on for me. A chance for her to get out of that restaurant once in a while. For you to think of me, I hope. Sean, who brings this to you, will show you how everything works.

I've enclosed the bookings diary as well as the phone I use for the ice cream business and, in order to make things easier for you, I've posted the change of keeper slip to the licence people so that Rosie is now registered in your name.

God bless and keep you, Lally.

Yours always,

Basil

Elle put her hand to her mouth. Swallowed. Her great-uncle. Family. He'd been within touching distance and she'd had no idea. She tried to remember serving someone on his own, but the Blue Boar had a motel that catered for businessmen travelling on their own.

Haughton Manor was only six or seven miles away but she had to get ready for work and there was no time to drive over there this evening. Find out more. Neither could she leave it and she reached for the phone, dialled Directory Enquiries.

'Lower Haughton, Basil Amery,' she said, made a note of the number and then dialled it.

After half a dozen rings it switched to voicemail. Had he already left? What events? Scandal, he'd mentioned in his letter… She left a message, asking him to call her—he'd pick up his messages even if he was away—left her number as well, and replaced the receiver. She was rereading his letter, trying to make sense of it, when the phone rang. She grabbed for it, hoping that he'd picked up the message and called back.

'Elle?'

It was her boss. 'Oh, hello, Freddy.'

'Don't sound so disappointed!'

'Sorry, I was expecting someone else. What's up?' she asked quickly, before he asked who.

'We're going to be short-staffed this evening. I was wondering if you can you drop everything and come in early.'

'Twenty minutes?' she offered.

'You're an angel.' Then, 'Would your sister be interested in doing a shift? She's a smart girl; she'd pick it up quickly enough. I'm sure she could use the money.'

'I'm sorry, Sorrel isn't here, but I was hoping for some more hours myself,' she added, taking advantage of a moment when he was the one asking for something.

'You already do more than enough. I'll have a word next time she drops in to the use the Wi-Fi. It wouldn't hurt her to help out.'

'She needs to concentrate...' But Freddy had already hung up and she was talking to herself.

She read the letter again, then replaced it in the envelope and put everything in the hall drawer. She didn't want her grandmother seeing the letter until Elle knew what the heck was going on.

There was nothing she could do with Rosie, but she'd be at work before anyone came home. She had until tomorrow morning to think of some good reason why it was parked in the drive.

Sean told himself that it was none of his business. That Basil was just a tenant who'd asked if he could keep Rosie at the barn since there wasn't a garage at the cottage.

He'd only got dragged into the situation because he'd stayed overnight in London on the day Basil decided to do his disappearing act. And if Lovage Amery had been a plain middle-aged woman Sean wouldn't have given the matter a first thought, let alone a second one.

Why Basil hadn't just decided to leave Rosie with him was the real mystery. She was safe enough locked up in the barn.

Unless, of course, he didn't intend to come back.

Or hadn't actually gone anywhere.

He swore, grabbed a spare set of keys from the estate safe and drove across the park to Keeper's Cottage.

He knocked, called out, then, when there was no answer, let himself in. Nothing seemed out of place. There were no letters ominously propped up on the mantelpiece. Only a photograph of a young woman wearing an outrageously short mini dress, white knee-length boots, her hair cut in a sharp angular style that had once been the height of fashion. Her large eyes were framed with thick sooty lashes and heavily lined. The gloss and polish, the expensive high fashion were as far from Lovage Amery as it was possible to be, and yet those eyes left him in no doubt about the family connection. Shape, colour were a perfect match.

So that was all right, then.

Basil must have had some bookings for Rosie that he couldn't cancel and was lumbering his family with the responsibility. If they weren't keen, it wasn't his problem.

The light was flashing on the answering machine and after a moment's hesitation he hit 'play'.

Lovage Amery's liquid voice filled the room. 'Mr Amery? My name is Lovage Amery and I've just read your letter. I don't understand. Who are you? Will you ring me? Please.' And she left a number.

Genuinely had no idea who Basil was? On the point of reaching for the phone, the phone in his pocket rang.

He checked the caller ID. Olivia.

'Sean, I'm at the barn,' she said before he could say a word. 'Where are you?'

The leap-to-it tone of the Haughton family, so different from the soft voice still rippling through him, evoking the memory of hot eyes that you could drown in. A dangerously appealing mouth. It was the kind of complicated response that should have sent up warning flares—*here be dragons*—but only made him want to dive right in.

Bad idea.

'I'm on the far side of the estate,' he said.

'It's nearly six.' His half-sister's pout was almost audible.

'You know how it is, sis,' he said, knowing how much she hated to be called that. 'No rest for younger illegitimate sons. Why are you here?'

'It's my home?'

'Excuse me? The last time you were here was Christmas. You stayed for two days, then abandoned your children with their nanny for the rest of the holidays while you went skiing.'

'They had a lovely time,' she protested.

Of course they had. He'd made sure of it, sliding down the hill on old tea trays in the snow, building dens, running wild as he had, in ways that were impossible in their urban lives in London. But they would still have rather been with their parents.

'Look, I don't want to fight with you, Sean. I wanted to talk about the stables. I want to convert them into craft workshops. I know all kinds of people—weavers, candle-makers, turners, who would fall over themselves for space. Visitors to the estate would love to see demonstrations. Buy stuff.'

He laughed.

'What's so funny?' she demanded.

'The idea that you would know what a turner did, let alone be acquainted with one.'

'Wretch. Henry thinks it's a good idea.'

'That would be Henry who visits his estate twice a year. At Christmas…' also to abandon his children before jetting off, although in his case to the Caribbean '…and for the shooting.' And for the occasional extramarital weekend in the same cottage his father had used for the purpose. Like father, like son.

'It's his estate, not yours,' she pointed out.

'So it is. And he pays me to run it professionally. At a profit.

Not as occupational therapy for women whose marriages are falling apart.'

Clearly she had no answer to that because she cut the connection without another word. That was one of the drawbacks of a mobile phone. You couldn't slam it down to make your point.

He replaced the photograph, took a thorough look around the cottage to make sure he hadn't overlooked anything. He found nothing to raise alarm signals but he was still vaguely uneasy. Regretted not staying at the Amerys' house to check the contents of Basil's envelope.

He hadn't taken much notice when Lovage Amery had initially denied any knowledge of Basil. He had family he'd deny in a heartbeat but that message on Basil's answering machine certainly hadn't sounded like a family call—even to family you didn't like. He'd heard enough of those over the years to recognise one when he heard it. She had been polite, businesslike but there had been no emotion. And if he was sure of anything, he was sure that Miss Lovage Amery was packed to the brim with that.

He'd be going that way this evening. Maybe he should call in to see her again. Just to put his mind at rest. Basil was, after all, his tenant and there were implications for the estate if he didn't intend to come back.

And, just in case Lovage Amery was still denying any family connection, he used his phone to take a picture of the photograph on the mantelpiece.

'Freddy...'
'Elle! You must have flown!' It was a good start but, before she could press her advantage and put her case for another shift, he said, 'Not now. All hands on deck.'

Rosie was exactly where he'd left her, which wasn't promising. Sean had hoped that whatever was in the envelope would have made things clear and she'd be tucked up safely behind the doors of what must once have been a carriage house. Taken into the fold, as it were.

As it was, he braced himself before ringing the doorbell. And not just because of the effect Lovage Amery had on his breathing.

Whatever the situation, after his park and ride performance this afternoon he wasn't anticipating a particularly warm welcome.

The deep breath was unnecessary. The door was opened by a teenage girl who was a vision in black. Black hair, black dress, black painted fingernails.

'Yes?' she demanded, with manners to match the clothes. 'What do you want?'

'A word with Lovage Amery?'

'What about?'

'Tell her it's Sean McElroy,' he said. 'She'll know.'

She shrugged. 'Gran, it's for you!' she shouted, hanging onto the door, keeping him on the step with the kind of stare that would frighten a zombie.

Gran? 'No…'

She waited, expressionless.

'Tall, dark hair, hazel eyes? No one's grandmother,' he added.

The green eyes in her deadpan face narrowed suspiciously. 'You want Elle?'

'Do I?' Elle?

'She's at work. She won't be home until late.'

'In that case, I'll come back tomorrow,' he said.

'Make it before eleven. She starts work at twelve,' she said, making a move to close the door.

'What is it, Geli?'

Sean looked beyond the black-garbed teen to the source of the voice. Walking towards him was the girl in Basil's photograph, over forty years on. Her hair had faded to grey and these days she wore it up in a soft chignon, but the eyes, even without the heavy fridge of false eyelashes, were unmistakable.

'It's okay, Gran. He doesn't want you, he wants Elle.'

'I hadn't realised there was more than one Lovage Amery,' Sean said quickly, bypassing the teen in favour of her grandmother, who was undoubtedly the intended recipient of Basil's envelope. 'Did Elle explain to you about Rosie?'

'Rosie?' she asked, confused. Which answered that question. 'Who's Rosie?'

'Not who, what. The ice cream van?'

'Oh, that. I wondered where it had come from. Is it yours?'

'No...' This was even harder than talking to Elle. 'I left a letter for you,' he prompted. 'From Basil?'

'Basil?' She took a step back, the graceful poise crumpling along with her face. 'No,' she whispered. 'He wouldn't. He mustn't. Bernard will be so angry...'

'Gran...' The girl, a protective arm around her grandmother, gave him a furious look and, for the second time that day, the front door of Gable End was shut firmly in his face.

Freddy stopped her with a touch to her arm. Elle's instincts were to pull away, but she reminded herself that he'd known her and her family since she was eighteen. That it was avuncular rather than familiar. He was, after all, old enough to be her uncle if not her father.

'There's a big party at the corner table, Elle. They've got drinks and should have had enough time to sort out what they want to eat by now. Will you take care of them?'

Only one of the backup staff had turned in and it had been non-stop since she'd arrived before six. She was due a break, but that wasn't going to happen and she pasted on a smile, took her book from her pocket and said, 'Of course, Freddy.'

The large round table in the corner could take up to a dozen people and it was full, which might mean a decent tip. Or a lot of work for nothing much. You could never tell.

Smile, Elle, smile, she told herself as she approached the

table. 'Are you ready to order?' she asked. 'Or do you need a little more…'

The words died away as she looked around the table and found herself face to face with Sean McElroy and her knees, already feeling the pressure from nearly three hours of non-stop action, momentarily buckled.

Since yelling at a diner, demanding to know why he'd dumped Rosie and run, would not improve her chances of a decent tip, she braced her knees, cleared her throat, said to no one in particular, 'If you need a little more time I can come back.'

'No, we're ready,' the man nearest to her said, acknowledging her with a smile before going around the table, so that she could keep her eyes on her notepad. Everything went smoothly until they reached Sean McElroy. 'Sean?' he prompted.

'Sorry, I can't make up my mind. I'm rather tempted by the chicken in a herb crust. Can you tell me exactly what the herbs are? Elle,' he added, proving that his vision was twenty-twenty too, since he could obviously read her name badge across the table.

So much for hoping to avoid another encounter with those blue eyes.

She looked up to find them fixed on her, his expression suggesting that she had some explaining to do which, under the circumstances, was some nerve.

The woman beside him, slender, cool in a linen shift of such simplicity that it had to have cost a mint, straight blonde hair shining like something out of a shampoo advert, turned to look at him and, instantly sensing that there was more going on than just a discussion about food, frowned.

'I thought you were going to have the steak, darling. You always have the steak,' she added, declaring herself in possession.

'Do I? I hadn't realised I was so boring, darling,' he said, keeping his eyes fixed resolutely on Elle. The 'darling' had sounded like an afterthought. Maybe the woman noticed that too, because she followed his gaze to Elle and her frown deepened.

'The crust consists of fine wholemeal breadcrumbs,' Elle rattled off quickly, 'and a mixture of fresh herbs including parsley, lemon thyme, a touch of sage, seasoned and bound together with egg.'

'No *lovage*?' he asked.

Well, she'd seen that one coming. Was ready for it. 'No lovage, no basil.' She waited, pencil poised.

'A pity. I'll have the salmon.'

She made a note, moved on. It was just another table, she told herself as she brought a jug of water, went around the table with a basket of warm rolls.

'Roll, madam?' she asked the blonde.

She shook her head.

She moved on 'Roll, sir?'

Sean looked up, his face so close to hers that she could see a thin jagged scar just above his eyebrow. Had he fallen off his bike when he was little? Been cut by something? Been hand-bagged by some woman he'd seriously annoyed?

He took his time deciding, then, when she'd finally picked out his choice with the tongs and she was congratulating herself on keeping her cool when all she wanted to do was crown him with them, he murmured, 'Tell me, Lovage, who is Bernard?' At which point the roll shot out of the tongs, knocked over a glass of water and in the confusion most of the rolls landed in his lap.

'One would have been sufficient,' he said, rescuing the basket and picking warm bread out of his lap, while she scrambled on the floor for the rest.

'Fetch fresh rolls, Elle. Quickly as you can.' Oh, no, Freddy *would* have to be looking… 'And replace this glass,' he added, handing it to her. 'I'm so sorry, everyone. Can I offer you fresh drinks? On the house, of course.'

'How about a fresh waitress. Someone in control of her hands. And her eyes,' the girl in the linen dress suggested, pointedly brushing away a few drops of water. 'My dress is ruined.'

'There is nothing wrong with the waitress,' Sean said as Freddy mopped up the spill, straightened the table.

'We can all see what *you* think of her—'

'The accident was entirely my fault,' he continued, speaking to Freddy, ignoring the woman at his side. 'And there's no need for fresh drinks. We're fine.'

Sean watched Lovage—Elle—Amery walk away and discovered that he wanted to go with her. Take her hand and walk out into the dusk with her. Walk across the village, along the towpath by the Common. Walk her home and kiss her on the step, ask her out on a date, just like they did in the old days.

'What did you say to her?' Charlotte demanded, intensifying the feeling.

'I asked for the roll with pumpkin seeds,' he replied.

'And you certainly got it,' someone chimed in. Everyone laughed except Charlotte.

'I don't believe you. You were flirting with her from the moment she came to the table,' she accused.

Sean realised that the restaurant owner was still hovering. Listening. 'If I was, then I am one hundred per cent to blame, because she certainly wasn't flirting back.' He forced himself to smile at the man. 'We're okay, really. Thanks.'

It was a dismissal and he took the hint, leaving them to their meal. Another waitress brought a fresh glass, a new basket of rolls, and served their meal, but he only had eyes for Elle as she weaved with drinks and trays of food between smaller tables on the far side of the room.

Reassigned out of the danger zone by the restaurant manager and no doubt happy to go.

What on earth had got into him?

He'd just taken his seat at the table when he'd looked around the room and seen her, hair restrained in a French plait, luscious curves neatly encased in a black shirt and trousers, a long black pinafore tied with strings around her waist.

She'd been laughing over a friendly exchange with a family she was serving at another table and he'd experienced another of those breath-stopping moments, just like the one he'd had when she'd opened the door to him.

He should have guessed this was where she worked.

There were a fairly limited number of jobs where she'd be working at this time of night, or on a Sunday lunchtime. A late-night garage, a twenty-four hour supermarket or a restaurant. And the Blue Boar—a rambling restaurant with bed and breakfast facilities for businessmen—was within walking distance of Gable End.

As he'd watched her, he saw the guy who'd shown them to their table, the one who'd come to see what the fuss was about, stop her with a hand to her arm as she'd passed him.

It looked familiar. Possessive.

As did the way the man's eyes had followed her as she came towards their table.

It was none of his business, he told himself. None at all. But then she'd looked up, seen him, and he just hadn't been able to stop himself.

Elle walked into the kitchen the following morning, gritty-eyed, heavy-limbed, late after a restless night with a head full of pink ice cream vans and blue-eyed men, to find it blissfully silent.

Sorrel had presumably walked her grandmother to church before going on to take advantage of the free Wi-Fi at the Blue Boar. And Geli would be doing an early turn, dog walking at the animal sanctuary.

She dropped the envelope and van keys she'd retrieved from the hall drawer onto the kitchen table, then opened the back door.

The sun poured in, bringing with it the song of a blackbird, the scent of the lilac and she lifted her face to the sun, feeling the life seep back as she breathed in the day. Breathed out the unpleasantness of last night. That girl with Sean McElroy might have been beautiful, elegant and polished, but beauty is as beauty does, at least that was what her grandmother always said.

She suspected that beauty like that could, and did, do whatever it pleased and Sean McElroy was clearly happy to let her.

Freddy had moved her to another table after the incident with the rolls. He had been quick to reassure her that he didn't blame her for what happened but, after all, the customer was always right.

It should have been a relief. *Was* a relief, she told herself. Between Sean and his girlfriend, someone would undoubtedly have had their dinner in their lap.

She had enough on her plate sorting out Rosie, without that kind of trouble. But not before she'd had a cup of tea and got some solid carbs inside her, she decided, picking up an elastic band from the bowl on the dresser and fastening back her hair.

She opened the bread bin.

Nothing but crumbs. And a shake told her that the cereal box on the table was empty.

She was on her knees hunting through the cupboards for the packet she'd bought the day before when a shadow cut off the sunlight.

It was too soon for her grandmother or Sorrel and she looked up expecting to see Geli, ready for a second helping of breakfast before going into Maybridge with her friends. And out of luck because the empty box on the table *was* the one she'd bought the day before.

But it wasn't Geli.

The silhouette blocking out the light was that of Pink Van Man himself, but only momentarily, since he didn't wait for an invitation but walked right in before she could ask him what the heck he thought he was doing.

A fast learner.

CHAPTER THREE

Life is uncertain. Eat dessert first.

—Rosie's Diary

SEAN MCELROY looked so much bigger, so much more dangerous now that she was on her knees. Maybe he was aware of that because he bent to offer her a hand up, enveloping her in a waft of something masculine that completely obliterated the scent of the lilac.

Old leather, motor oil, the kind of scents unknown in an all female household, and she found herself sucking it in like a starving kitten.

Her eyes were level with a pair of narrow hips, powerful thighs encased in soft denim, closer to a man—at least one she wanted to be close to—than she'd been since she'd said goodbye to her dreams and taken a job working unsocial hours.

'How did you get in?' she demanded.

'The gate was open.'

Oh, great. She nagged about security but no one took her seriously. Except, of course, it wasn't about that.

Leaving the gate open was Geli's silent protest against Elle's flat refusal to take in any more four-footed friends, no matter how appealing. Why bother to shut the gate when there was no dog to keep off the road?

She shook him off, cross, hot and bothered. 'It's not an invitation for anyone to walk in,' she snapped, standing up without assistance.

'No? Just as well I closed it then,' he said. 'It could do with a new lock.'

'I could do with any number of new things, Mr McElroy. The one thing I *don't* need is an old van. Can I hope that your arrival means you've realised your mistake and have come to take her home?'

'Sorry,' he said.

'You don't look it.' He wasn't smiling exactly, but she was finding it hard to hold onto her irritation.

'Would it help if I said that I honestly believed you were expecting her?'

'Really?' she enquired. 'And what part of "Go away and take Rosie with you" didn't you understand?'

He ignored the sarcasm. 'I thought that once you'd opened the envelope it would make sense.'

'So why are you here now?'

He shrugged. 'I'm not sure. Just a feeling that something's not quite right. Did Basil leave a note?' he asked, nodding in the direction of the envelope. 'I'm a bit concerned about him.'

'But not about me, obviously. Your little stunt last night could have cost me my job. Did you enjoy your salmon?' she accused.

'I have to admit that the evening went downhill right after you dumped a basket of hot rolls in my lap,' he said.

'I hope you're not expecting an apology.'

'No. I take it you didn't get the message I left for you?'

He'd left a message? She shook her head. 'We were rushed off our feet last night. I didn't hang around to chat.'

'No?' There was something slightly off about the way he said that.

'Would you?' she asked. 'After six hours on your feet?'

'It depends what was on offer.'

She frowned and he shook his head. 'No, forget it. I'm sorry if you got into trouble but you have to admit that while you might not know Basil, the name Bernard certainly makes you all jump.'

'All?'

'Your grandmother nearly passed out when I asked her if she'd had Basil's letter,' he explained.

'Gran? Are you telling me that you came back here yesterday? After I'd gone to work?'

'I called in on my way to the Blue Boar. I did tell the skinny vampire that I'd come back this morning,' he said.

'Geli…' She smothered a grin. 'I haven't seen her this morning. I've only just got up. What did Gran say?'

'She wasn't exactly coherent, but I think the gist was that Bernard wouldn't allow her to receive a letter from Basil. She seemed panic-stricken at the thought.'

'Well, that's just ridiculous. Bernard was my grandfather but he's been dead for years,' she told him.

And yet there was obviously something. It was there in the letter.

'Tell me about him,' she said.

'Basil?' He shrugged. 'I don't know much. He's just an old guy with two passions in his life. Rosie and poker.'

'He's a gambler? Are you saying that he puts Rosie up as surety for his bets?'

'He'd never risk losing Rosie,' he assured her. Then added, 'Which is not to say that if he got into trouble some of his playing partners wouldn't take her in lieu if they could get their hands on her.'

'So, what are you saying? That you've been appointed getaway driver and I've been chosen to give her sanctuary?' *It… not she.* She was doing it now. But it explained why Basil had gone to the bother of registering her grandmother as Rosie's keeper.

'That's about the gist of it,' he admitted, stretching his neck, easing his shoulders.

'Don't do that!' she said as his navy polo shirt rippled, offering a tantalising promise of the power beneath the soft jersey. Talk about distraction…

Sean frowned. He didn't have a clue what she was talking about, thank goodness.

'Does he disappear regularly?' she asked before he had time to work it out.

'I wouldn't know. I'm his landlord, not his best buddy. But he garages Rosie with me and I was in London when he took off and he couldn't get in. It would seem that his need to disappear was too urgent to wait until morning.'

'So, what? He dropped a note through your letter box asking you to bring her here?'

'I'm sorry about that,' he said, looking slightly uncomfortable, no doubt thinking that she was taking a dig at him for doing the same. 'I assumed that once you'd read whatever was in the envelope you'd know what to do.'

What to do?

It got worse, she thought, suddenly realising exactly what this was all about.

'I'm sorry, Sean, but if you've come here expecting to be paid your rent, you're out of luck. I don't know Basil Amery and, even if I did, I couldn't help you. You're going to have to sell Rosie to recover your losses.'

'Sell Rosie? Are you kidding?'

'Obviously,' Elle said, back to sarcasm. 'Since she's Basil's pride and joy.'

'You don't sound convinced.'

'I can think of more important things to lavish your love on. I mean, how would you react to someone you've never heard of expecting you to run an ice cream round for him?'

Sean thought about it for a moment, then said, 'Why don't I put the kettle on? I make a mean cup of coffee.'

'I haven't got any coffee,' she said, tucking a wayward strand of hair behind her ear.

'Tea, then,' he said, picking up the kettle, filling it and turning it on. He took a couple of mugs off the dresser and since the tea bags were stored in a tin with 'TEA' on the front—life was complicated enough without adding to the confusion—he found them without making a mountain out of a molehill. So far, he was doing better than either of her sisters ever managed. 'Milk, sugar?' he asked, dropping a bag in each mug.

She wanted to tell him to go and take the van with him, but he was right. They needed to get to the bottom of this.

'Just a dash of milk.'

Was there any milk?

'How about sugar? You've obviously had a shock.'

'Of course I haven't,' she said, pulling herself together. 'This is some kind of weird mistake. It has to be.'

They weren't the most conventional family in the world, but they didn't have secrets. Quite the contrary. Anyone would give him chapter and verse…

He glanced back to her.

'What are you so scared of, Elle?'

'I'm not scared!'

'No?'

'No!' She'd faced the worst that the world could throw at her, but he was right, something about this put her on edge and, seizing on the fact that the kettle hadn't come on to divert his attention, she said, 'You have to give the plug a wiggle.'

He wasn't diverted, just confused, and she reached behind him.

'Don't!' Sean said as he realised what she was doing. He made a lunge in her direction, but not in time to stop her. There was a bit of a crackle and a tiny shock rippled up her arm, then the light came on and the kettle began to heat up noisily.

Her cheeks lit up to match but the rush of heat that invaded her body, starting at the spot where his hand was fastened over hers was, fortunately, silent.

Or maybe not.

Maybe the hammering of her pulse in her ears was so loud that Sean could hear it too, because he dropped her hand so fast that you'd have thought she was the one with dodgy wiring.

Without a word, he took a wooden spoon from the pot by the stove, used the handle to switch off the kettle and then removed the plug from the socket.

Whatever. Tea had been his idea.

But he wasn't done. Having disconnected the kettle, he began opening the dresser drawers.

'Excuse me!'

He held up a screwdriver he'd found in the drawer that contained bits of string, paper bags, the stuff that didn't have any other home.

'It's beyond help,' she told him. 'It's just…' worn out, past its use by date, just plain old '…vintage. Like Rosie.'

'It's nothing like Rosie,' he said, ignoring her protest as he set about taking the plug apart. 'Rosie is not an accident waiting to happen.'

'That's a matter of opinion,' she retorted.

'No. It's a matter of fact. She's completely roadworthy or I wouldn't be driving her.' He looked up. 'And I wouldn't have brought her to you.'

'No?' Then, realising just how rude she was being, she blushed. 'No, of course not. Sorry…'

'No problem.'

'I'm glad you think so,' she said, only too aware of the envelope that was lying on the kitchen table with all the appeal of an unexploded bomb.

The Amery family had lived at Gable End for generations. This was the house Grandpa had been born in and it was marked with traces of everyone who'd ever lived there.

Their names were written in the fly-leaves of books that filled shelves in almost every room. Were scratched into the handles of ancient tennis racquets, stencilled onto the lids of old school trunks in the attic.

Their faces as babies, children, brides and grooms, soldiers, parents, grandparents, filled photograph albums.

There was no Basil.

Okay, there were gaps. Photographs fell out, were borrowed, lost.

Or had some been removed?

Gran had recognised the name. According to Sean, she hadn't acted in the slightly silly, coy way she did when some man from the pensioners' club chatted her up, and they often did because she was still beautiful.

She'd nearly passed out, he'd said. Panicked. And then there was Basil's letter. He'd mentioned Bernard and referred to him as 'my brother'. The connection was definitely there. Maybe she just didn't want to believe it.

Taking a deep breath, she picked up the envelope—no one called her a scaredy-cat—and tipped the contents out onto the table so that he could see that she wasn't trying to hide anything.

'Here's Basil's letter,' she said, offering it to Sean, who was leaning against the dresser, still poking about in the plug with the screwdriver. 'You'd better read it,' she said, thrusting it at him before turning her attention to the notebook.

On the first page, where a printed note said *'In case of loss, please return to:'* the word 'ROSIE' had been written in block capitals, along with a mobile phone number. Presumably belonging to the phone on the table.

It was a page-a-day diary, she discovered, as she riffled through the pages, hoping for some clue. To the man. To his whereabouts.

There were appointments with names and telephone numbers by them. The occasional comment. Quotes by the famous, as well as Basil's own wry or funny comments on the joys of ice cream. There were only a couple of recent entries.

'He's written "RSG" on yesterday's date. Underlined. Do you know anyone with those initials?'

He thought about it for a moment, then shook his head.

'That's it, apart from "Service, Sean" written in the space for last Friday. Are you a mechanic? There's a collection of vintage cars at Haughton Manor, isn't there? Do you take care of them?'

'They come under my care,' he said. 'Basil asked if I'd change Rosie's oil, run a few basic checks to make sure everything was in good shape since he had some bookings. His back has been playing him up,' he added, almost defensively. Doing little jobs on the side that his boss didn't know about? Not her concern.

'How much does he pay you?' she asked. The last thing she needed was an elderly—vintage—vehicle that required high level, high cost maintenance, but she didn't appear to have much choice in the matter. The mystery remained, but the connection between Basil and her family appeared to be proved.

He shrugged and a smile teased at the corner of his mouth, creating a tiny ripple of excitement that swept through her, overriding her irritation, and it occurred to her that a man like Sean McElroy could be seriously good for her state of mind.

'Basil prefers to give payment in kind,' he said.

'Ice cream?' She looked at him. The narrow hips, ropey arms. Her state of mind and all points south. 'How much ice cream can one man eat?'

'Fortunately, I don't have to eat it all myself. He brought Rosie along to a family birthday party fully loaded with ice cream and toppings. The brownie points I earned for that were worth their weight in brake liners.'

'Family? You have children?'

'No. The party was for my niece. Half-niece.' He shrugged. 'I have a complicated family.'

'Don't we all,' she said wryly. 'But that's a lot of ice cream for one little girl's birthday.'

'It was a big party. My family don't do things by halves,' he said.

'No?' They had that in common, only in her case it tended to be dramas rather than celebrations. 'How do you know him?'

'Basil? He's a tenant on the Haughton Manor estate.'

'Keeper's Cottage. It's on the vehicle logbook,' she said. 'It's so near. I went there once on a school trip when we were doing the Tudors. It's beautiful.'

'So people keep telling me.'

'You live there too?' she asked.

'Live there, work there, for my sins. Or, rather, my mother's,' he said, before returning to the letter. 'Lally? Is that what people call your grandmother?'

'Yes.' She'd much rather hear about his mother's sins, but he'd changed the subject so emphatically that she didn't pursue it. 'I doubt many people know her real name.'

'Or yours?'

'Or mine,' she admitted.

'Well, Basil certainly does, and he's got a photograph of her on his mantelpiece to prove it.'

'You're kidding! A picture of my grandmother?'

He took a phone from his pocket, clicked through it and held it out to her. 'I took this yesterday when I let myself in. Just to be sure that he hadn't done anything…foolish.'

'Killed himself, you mean?' she said pointedly.

He didn't answer but that was what he'd meant. It was why he was here now. Why he'd wanted to see the letter.

'You have his keys?' she asked.

'Not personally. There are master keys in the estate safe. For emergencies.'

'Or when a tenant does a runner,' she said, taking the phone from him.

'It is her?' he asked about the woman in the photo.

She nodded. 'It was taken in the late sixties, before she married my grandfather.'

Her grandmother had been the height of fashion with her dark hair cut in a sharp chin-length bob by a top London stylist, her huge eyes heavily made-up, her lips pale. And the dress she was wearing was an iconic Courrèges original design.

She handed it back to him. 'How did you know this was gran?'

'I didn't until I saw her last night, but it was obvious she was related to you. The likeness is unmistakable.'

'But she was...'

She stopped. Her grandmother had been the pampered daughter of the younger son of the Earl of Melchester. A debutante. An acknowledged beauty.

One of the girls in pearls who'd featured in the pages of *Country Life*.

While the Amerys were a solid middle-class family, it hadn't been the marriage her father had planned for his daughter. No minor aristocracy to offer inherited wealth, park gates, maybe a title, so Elle's grandmother had been pretty much cut adrift from her family when she'd married Bernard Amery.

'I don't look a bit like her,' she said instead.

'Not superficially, maybe, but you have her mouth. Her eyes. Basil recognised you,' he pointed out. He looked again at the letter. 'Is your grandmother about?' he asked.

'No!' She shook her head. 'You can't bother her with this, Sean.'

'You haven't shown her the letter?'

'Not yet.' Once her grandmother had read it, Elle would be well and truly lumbered. And not just with an old crock that would cost a fortune to tax, insure, keep running. There were the obligations, too.

Oh, no, wait.

The connection had been made. He knew he'd brought Rosie to the right place and as far as Sean McElroy was concerned there was nothing more to be said.

She was already lumbered.

It was true, nothing good ever came out of a brown envelope. Well, this time it wasn't going to happen. She wasn't going to let it.

Whatever her grandmother had done for him in the past, Basil was going to have to sort out his own problems. They had quite enough of their own.

'They seem to have been very close,' he said, looking again at the letter. 'He says she saved his life.'

'He'd have had a job to end it all in the village pond,' she told him dryly. 'No matter what time of day or night, someone would be sure to spot you.'

'Your grandmother, in this case. No doubt it was just a cry for help, but she seems to have listened. Sorted him out.'

Her ditzy, scatterbrained grandmother?

'If that's the case, why haven't they seen one another for forty years? Unless...' She looked up. 'If she married his brother, maybe they fell out over her. She was very beautiful.'

'Yes...'

'Although why would Grandpa have removed every trace of his brother's presence from the family home? After all, he got the girl,' she mused.

'Of course he got the girl. Basil is gay, Elle.'

'Gay?' she repeated blankly.

'Could that be the reason his family disowned him?' Sean asked.

'No!' It was too horrible to imagine. 'They wouldn't.'

'People do. Even now.'

'They weren't like that,' she protested.

Were they?

Sean was right. Forty years was a lifetime ago. She had no idea how her great-grandparents would have reacted to the news that one of their sons was gay. Or maybe she did. Basil had mentioned his mother in the letter. If she'd still been alive, he'd said...

You could change the law but attitudes took longer, especially among the older generation.

As for her grandfather, Bernard, he'd been a slightly scary stranger, someone who'd arrived out of the blue every six months or so, who everyone had to tiptoe around. Breathing a collective sigh of relief when he disappeared overseas to do whatever he did in Africa and the Middle East.

'Whatever happened, Gran can't be bothered with this. She's not strong, Sean.'

As always, it was down to her. And the first thing she'd have to do was go through the diary and cancel whatever arrangements Basil had made. If she could work out what they were.

'What does this mean?' she asked, flicking through the notebook again.

Sean didn't answer and she looked up, then wished she hadn't because he was looking straight at her and those blue eyes made her a little giddy. She wanted to smile, grab him and dance. Climb aboard Rosie and ring her bell.

She took a deep breath to steady herself.

'It says "Sylvie. PRC" Next Saturday'?' she prompted, forcing herself to look away.

'PRC? That'll be the Pink Ribbon Club. It's a charity supporting cancer patients and—' He paused as he tightened the final screw in the plug.

'And their families,' she finished for him, the words catching in her throat. 'I know.'

'It's their annual garden party on Saturday. They're holding it at Tom and Sylvie MacFarlane's place this year.'

'Where's that?'

'Longbourne Court.'

'Oh, yes, of course. I'd heard it was occupied at last.'

'I saw the signs advertising the garden party when I passed the gates. Basil mentioned it when he asked me to change Rosie's oil. I got the feeling he'd volunteered to help because it meant something special to him.'

'He should have thought of that before he bet the farm on the turn of a card,' she said, suddenly angry with this man who appeared to have absolutely no sense of responsibility. Worse. Didn't have the courage to face them and ask for help, but left someone else to do his dirty work. 'But then, from his letter, he appears to have made a life's work of letting people down.'

'You're assuming that it's a gambling problem.'

'You were the one who mentioned it as a possibility,' she reminded him.

'Grasping at straws? Maybe that was the problem with his family,' he suggested. 'Maybe he'd flogged the family silver to pay his creditors.'

'Not guilty,' she said, earning herself a sharp look. 'And I thought you said it was a recent problem?'

'He's been living on the estate for less than a year, so what do I know? Maybe he only gambles when he's unhappy. A form of self-harming?'

No, no, no... She wasn't listening.

'I can't have Gran involved in anything like this, Sean.'

'All he's asking is that she—or, rather, you—keeps Rosie's business ticking over.'

'Is it?'

'That's what he put in the note he left me.' He looked again at the letter to her grandmother. 'This does make it sound rather more permanent, I have to admit.'

'Well, whatever he wants, it's impossible. I have a job that keeps me fully occupied and Gran doesn't have a driving licence,' she protested, clutching at straws. 'Besides, her concentration isn't that great. She'd think it was all a wonderful treat and give all the ice cream away. Or just wander off when she got bored.'

'Is it Alzheimer's?' he asked point-blank.

'No.' She shook her head. 'She always had a bit of a reputation for giddiness but she's had a lot to deal with over the years. She blamed herself for Grandpa's death, which is ridiculous,' she added, before he could start adding two and two and making five. 'He was killed in a road accident. In Nigeria. And then my mother died. She hasn't been quite focused since then. Her doctor thinks she simply blocks out what she can't cope with.'

'We all have days when we'd like to do that,' he murmured sympathetically.

'Yes...' Then, afraid that she was revealing more than

she should, 'You can see why I won't have her put under any stress.'

'Of course,' he said. 'But there's absolutely nothing wrong with your focus, Lovage. Maybe, since you've taken charge of the letter meant for her, you could at least stand in for your grandmother on Saturday.'

CHAPTER FOUR

There's nothing wrong with life that a little ice cream won't fix.

—Rosie's Diary

ELLE should have seen that coming.

'Didn't you hear me?' she said. 'I work on Saturdays.'

'Not until the evening and the garden party will be over by six. There's going to be a concert in the grounds in the evening,' he added, in case she needed convincing. 'I promise you it'll be more fun than waiting tables.'

'Really? On my feet all day dishing out ice cream to fractious children? Irritable adults. Nobody with the right change. Can you positively guarantee that?'

He grinned without warning. 'You're weakening, I can tell.'

It was hard not to grin right back at his cheek, but she made an effort.

'I'm not, but even if I was beginning to crack, we have another problem. I haven't a clue how to work one of those ice cream machines.'

'It's not rocket science. I'll show you.'

'You?'

Her heart gave a little flutter. She hadn't anticipated that he would stick around to help and she was almost tempted.

'Who do you think was filling the cones at my niece's party while Basil was chatting up all the yummy mummies?'

She rather suspected that the yummy mummies were lining up to flirt with Sean, and she was equally sure that he would have been flirting back.

'Well, there you are,' she said, trying not to care about the fact that she was simply one in a long, meaningless line of women who had been suckered by that smile. Reminding herself that he was already spoken for by the cool blonde from the restaurant. 'Problem solved.' He knew how the equipment worked and a smile, a body like that, would be very good for business. 'If you think it's such fun, then Rosie is all yours.' She offered him the diary and the keys. 'Have a lovely day.'

He grinned. 'There's no doubt about it. You and Basil are definitely kin.'

'Then you must know that you are stuffed. Nice meeting you, Sean. Don't forget to shut the gate on your way out.'

'Nice try, but I don't think so.' He folded his arms, leaned back. Going nowhere. 'If you won't do it, I'll just have to wait here until your grandmother comes home. Where is she?' He glanced at his watch. 'Church?'

'Sean!'

'Or I could run you through the basics now,' he said. 'Give you that spin around the village so that you can get a feel for her.'

So much for appealing to his better nature. Clearly, he didn't have one. 'This is blackmail,' she said severely.

'You do drive?'

She was tempted to tell a flat out lie and say no. Perhaps it was as well for her immortal soul that he didn't wait for her to answer.

'Only I couldn't help noticing that you have a rather lovely old car in the garage and if Grannie can't drive...?'

'I didn't say she couldn't drive. I said she didn't have a licence. The result of one too many speeding tickets. And it's not a lovely old car, it's a heap of junk beyond help according to the guy at the garage when it failed its MOT. I'm sorry, Sean, but the last thing I need is more useless transport.'

'Rosie isn't useless.'

'She is to me. Or maybe you're suggesting I start an ice cream round to cover the cost of a trip to the supermarket?'

'Why not?' he asked. 'I'd stop you and buy one any time.'

The words were out of Sean's mouth before he could stop them.

There were women in this world who, you knew at a glance, you should not just walk, but run away from. The ones who still blushed, who looked at you with everything they were thinking plain to read in their eyes, whose hearts had not yet built up a protective layer of scar tissue.

Old-fashioned women who believed in love and marriage and family. The kind of woman a man, if he believed in none of those things, flirted with at his peril.

He had just stepped over an invisible line and they both knew it.

Elle covered the moment, lifting her arms, removing the band from which her hair was slipping, refastening it in one smooth movement. His fingers itched to reach out and stop her, slide his fingers through it. Tell her she should leave it loose.

One step, two steps...

'Do you think Basil means to come back, Sean?' she asked, breaking the spell. 'You said you were concerned about him and that letter did sound very much like goodbye.'

He wanted to reassure her, but the fact that Basil had gone to the lengths of transferring ownership of his most treasured possession to a woman he hadn't seen in forty years had a certain finality about it.

'Your guess is as good as mine,' he said, meeting her gaze, acknowledging the unasked question. 'I'm simply following Basil's script.'

'And you're doing a fine job. Unfortunately, you appear to be in a one-man show.'

'I'd noticed.'

'Isn't there some kind of retirement home for old vehicles like Rosie?' she asked a touch desperately. 'Somewhere you could put her out to grass?'

And, just like that, the tension went out of him and he was struggling to hold back a smile. 'Like an old donkey?' he suggested.

'Yes… No! You know what I mean!'

'I know what you mean,' he confirmed, not bothering to hide his amusement as she dissolved into blushing confusion, 'but I think you'll find that in automotive circles they're known as scrapyards.'

'It's all just a joke to you, isn't it?' she demanded and just as swiftly the confusion was gone.

She was still pink, but it was anger driving her now. She was an emotional hotspot. Trouble. Delightful. Dangerous.

'You told me that she's vintage. Isn't that special?' she demanded. 'What about a transport museum?'

Elle knew she was clutching at straws but, between Grandpa's old crock in the garage and now the van, she was beginning to feel like a serial vehicle murderer.

'Somewhere boys—grown-up boys like Basil, and you—can go and drool over her?' she persisted.

'This is where Basil chose, Elle. He specifically wanted you and your grandmother to have her.'

'Why? If he thinks Gran is so great, why didn't he come and visit? Ask us for help if he needed it? We haven't got any money and the menu runs to chickpeas more often than chicken but we've got plenty of room. If he's family—' If? Was there any doubt? 'If he's family, we would have taken care of him.'

'Would you?'

'We're not exactly overburdened with relatives. He might not have needed us, but did it never occur to him that we might have needed him? When Grandpa died. When my mother died.' When the sky fell in. 'What was his *problem*?'

He shrugged again, drawing quite unnecessary attention once more to the kind of shoulders that any red-blooded woman would be happy rubbing against as she filled cones with cool, sweet ice cream. She could do with an ice right now to cool her off.

'Sorry,' he said. 'You'll have to ask the other Lovage to fill you in on the family secrets.'

'I can't do that.' Who knew what memories would be dredged up from Gran's confused brain if it was brought up now, when it could do no good? What harm it might do. 'You saw her, Sean. Something really bad happened here decades ago and I'm not going to be the one to bring it all back.'

'Which answers your question about why Basil hasn't come to you for help in forty years.' She swallowed. 'She saw Rosie last night,' he said, pushing her. 'She's going to want to know where she came from,' he warned.

'No, she's not, because you're going to take her back where she came from.'

Sean took another look at the letter. '"Lavender's girls"?' he queried, ignoring her desperate interjection. 'Lavender is your mother?'

'Was. She died.'

'So it's just you and the black moth?' he asked.

'Geli?' She stifled a laugh at his description. Kinder than 'skinny vampire', but not by much. 'Angelica,' she added by way of explanation. 'She's sixteen. There's Sorrel, too. She's just started at college.'

'Lovage, Lavender, Angelica, Sorrel... The horticultural theme continues. When did your mother die?'

'When I was the age Geli is now. It was cancer,' she said before he asked. 'The virulent kind that comes with the death sentence included in the diagnosis. And, before you ask, there is no on\e else. It's just the four of us.'

Suddenly her throat was achingly thick and her eyes were stinging. Why had he come here, raking up the past? Making her remember?

'Is there any danger of that cup of tea you promised me?' she asked.

'Just as soon as I've fixed this kettle. Why don't you go and sit in the garden?' he suggested with a touch to her shoulder. 'I'll bring it out.'

Elle would rather have stayed right where she was, moving into the comfort promised by that hand, rather than away from it. To be held, feel the warmth of an arm around her, rather than being given another cup of the eternally cheering tea. Maybe he recognised the need in her eyes because he turned abruptly away to plug in the kettle. Elle backed off, fled outside, pulling a heavy raceme of lilac down, burying her face in the sweetness of it, just as she'd seen her mother do. She'd never understood why she did that.

It wasn't an elusive scent that you had to seek out. It filled the garden and up close was almost overpowering but right now she needed it in her lungs, in her heart. Needed it to smother the painful memories that Sean's arrival had stirred up.

Despite what she'd said, she knew she was going to have to take Rosie. Not for Basil. He was no different from every other man who'd touched her life. Just one more man who'd messed up and then run away.

Her grandfather had gone through the motions, done all the right things, but all at arm's length. He'd rarely been home and when he was there were no hugs, only a laughter-dampening gloom.

As for Basil, he hadn't cared enough about them to come and see if 'Lavender's girls' were all right. To pitch in and be a father figure—a grandfatherly figure—in their lives, when they'd needed one most.

Maybe that was why her mother had subconsciously sought out here-today-gone-next-week men, choosing relationships with built-in obsolescence. Choosing children whose love was unconditional, rather than some man whose presence cast a dark shadow.

Elle had welled up when she'd read that letter but it was phoney self-pitying sentiment. How could it be anything else when she didn't know Basil?

She did, however, know the Pink Ribbon Club and she owed them a lot more than a van full of ice cream.

One day out of her life was little enough in return for the kindness, the care they'd given her mother, easing her through her last days. And not just her mother. They'd been there for her grandmother, for three girls whose lives were falling apart, when there was no one else.

She'd always promised herself she would give something back when she had the time, the money to do so, and here she was, being offered the chance to do something positive to help raise funds so that other families could benefit as hers had done.

'Watch out!' Sean said as she stepped back, stumbled into him.

'Sorry.'

'No damage,' he said, sucking on his thumb where the tea had slopped over, drawing attention to his mouth. The crease bracketing one corner. 'Come on,' he said, looking up and catching her. 'I'll introduce you to Rosie.'

She knew what he was doing. It was no doubt what he'd planned from the moment he suggested she sit outside.

This was Geli's stray dog all over again.

'Just look at her, Elle…'

Her sister had known that once she'd seen the poor wretch she wouldn't be able to say no, and Sean was using the same tactics.

Look at this cute pink van. How can you resist?

He didn't wait, but headed for the gate, taking her tea with him. And the garden seemed emptier, flatter without him, as if he was somehow generating the buzzy atmosphere that raised her heart rate in a way that no amount of scrubbing could match.

At the gate he turned back. 'I'll give you the guided tour.'

Boom, boom, boom…

A buzz like an electric charge ran up her arm as he placed a hand at her elbow, supporting her over the worn path as if she didn't manage it all by herself at least twice a day. She should object. Tell him to keep his hands to himself. Except for that she'd have to be able to get her lips, tongue and teeth in a row to form the words. And then make her mouth say them.

Sean, on the other hand, was more likely keeping close contact in case she took the chance to shut and bolt the gate after him. Which was what she should have done. Would have done if she had any sense. But everyone knew that sense wasn't something Amery women were blessed with.

Despite the fact that she hadn't put a foot wrong in the seven years since she'd become the responsible one, she knew that the entire village was watching her. Waiting for the other shoe to drop.

For years they'd held their collective breath whenever the fair arrived in the village and dangerous young men flexed their muscles at the local girls.

They hadn't a clue...

Sean took the keys from his pocket, opened up the front door and reached in. A loud, slightly tinny rendition of 'Greensleeves' filled the air.

'No!' she exclaimed.

Too late. Before he could switch it off, a voice called out, 'You found him, I see.'

She swung around, her heart sinking as she saw Mrs Fisher peering over the fence, her attention fixed not on Rosie, but on the man at her side. The old witch had probably been keeping watch for him ever since yesterday afternoon. The ice cream chime, brief though it had been, had given her all the excuse she needed to dash out and take a second look.

'I asked Elle if she was starting an ice cream round,' she explained to Sean with a little laugh.

'Rosie is a bit too old for that kind of excitement,' he said. 'She's available for events, though. Parties. Weddings.'

Elle glared at him.

He handed her a mug of tea before taking a sip from his own.

'Parties? Well, that is interesting.' Mrs Fisher's eyes were wide as she took in every detail of Sean's appearance, storing it up to pass on, along with the news that he appeared to be very much at home in the Amery kitchen. 'You should put a notice up in the village shop, er…' She paused, waiting for Sean to fill in his name.

'I don't think that will be necessary,' Elle said before he could oblige her.

'You've got plenty of bookings, then?' she pressed.

'More than I can handle,' she assured her, keeping the polite distant smile on her face, the one that long experience had taught her was the only way to blank the busybodies.

'Well, that is good news!' She continued to look hopefully at Sean, but he'd taken the hint and, when it became obvious that neither of them were going to elaborate, the other woman said, 'Well, I must get on.'

'I'll bet you must,' Elle muttered as she watched her scurry up the road.

'Did I miss something?' Sean asked, putting his mug down on the windowsill.

'You might,' she told him, 'but she won't have. Why on earth did you tell her that Rosie was available for parties?'

'Because she is. Basil gave you free rein in his letter and, believe me, it's a lot more fun than being polite to the likes of me at the Blue Boar,' he said.

'No doubt,' she said with feeling, 'but not everyone is as much trouble as you. Or as rude as your girlfriend. And at least I'm guaranteed the minimum wage plus tips. How many bookings are there in Basil's diary?'

'I've no idea. Maybe you shouldn't have been so quick to rubbish the lady's advice about putting up a notice in the village store,' he jibed.

'That's no lady,' she muttered, 'that's Mrs Fisher. And when I said it wouldn't be necessary, it was because by tomorrow everyone within a five mile radius of Longbourne will know that I have an ice cream van parked in my drive and a man making free with my kettle.'

'That constitutes hot news in Longbourne?' he asked curiously.

'The hottest.' She lifted a shoulder, took a swig of the tea he'd brought her. He'd added sugar. She never used it, but maybe he was right about shock because it tasted wonderful. 'The jungle drums will be beating right now and within minutes the postmistress will be marking the date on the calendar. Starting the countdown.'

He frowned.

'Nine,' she prompted. 'Eight, seven...'

He muttered a word that wasn't quite six.

'To be fair,' she elaborated, 'we have history. My mother had a weakness for travelling men. The fact that all three of us have birthdays in late February is not a coincidence.'

He thought about it for a moment. 'You were all conceived in June?'

'He doesn't just make a mean cup of tea, he does mental arithmetic too.'

'No point in making a rubbish one. That was the last of the milk, by the way. I'll run you to the village shop in Rosie if you like. There's nothing like a live appearance to generate publicity.'

'That would give the old biddies a thrill.'

And not just the old biddies. Just the thought of being tucked up alongside him in Rosie sent a ripple of heat that had nothing to do with hot, sweet tea racing recklessly through her veins. And if you were going to get talked about anyway...

'I'm here to serve.'

Oh, yes!

'So what happens in June?' he asked.

She blinked. 'June?' For a moment her brain freewheeled before she managed to get A grip, engage the cogs, start thinking. 'The first week is the highlight of the Longbourne calendar. The only highlight,' she added wryly.

'The fair?'

'I never go myself. I just stand on the sidelines looking at the men putting up the rides, erecting the stalls.'

'Searching for a likeness?' he commented thoughtfully.

No doubt about it, he was good at mental arithmetic. Give him two and two and he came up with a neat four, no problem.

'I know it's stupid,' she said sadly. 'I mean, what would I say? You don't know me but I think you might have met my mother twenty-four years ago?'

'Actually,' he replied, 'I think it's far more likely that some man would look up, see you with the sun shining on your hair and remember a long ago summer interlude with a beautiful woman. Wish he was still young.'

She put the mug down on a low wall before she spilled her tea. Compliments were a rare commodity in her life and that one took her breath away. Then, aware that she was making a prize fool of herself and needing to get a grip, fast, she said, 'No awkward pregnancy or morning sickness to mar the memory for him.'

'What can I say?'

'You don't have to say anything. My mother was no poster woman for safe sex. Not much of an example to her daughters.'

In truth, she suspected that, as far as the village was concerned, Elle had been a real disappointment in terms of being gossip fodder but, with the house to take care of, Gran and two younger sisters to keep on the straight and narrow, as well as having to work to keep them all fed, she hadn't had a lot of time or cash to waste on the temptations of the Longbourne Fair. Temptations of any kind. Her life was on hold for the foreseeable future and the village biddies had shifted their attention to Sorrel once she'd hit puberty. No luck there, either. She was totally focused on her studies—she didn't want to end up like her big sister in a dead end job—to give them anything to gossip about.

But this year Angelica was looking promising. Sixteen was such a dangerous age and, obsessed with Dracula, she'd dyed her hair black, wore the palest make-up she could find and wore scarlet lipstick when she could get away with it.

Not that any age was safe for Amery women, as she'd found out when that Court Summons had arrived just after she'd started her first term at the local college.

Her hair was slipping from an elastic band that had lost its twang. Out of control, a bit like her. She gave it a sharp tug to restore order. Fat chance. Like her day, her week, her life it disintegrated in her hand.

'Drat,' she said as her hair collapsed untidily about her face and shoulders, digging around in her pocket to find another one, coming up empty-handed. 'It really needs cutting.'

'No.' Sean's smile faded as he lifted a handful, letting it run through his fingers. 'Believe me, it really doesn't. It's perfect just the way it is.'

CHAPTER FIVE

The perfect ice cream is like the perfect woman: cool, delicate, subtle, with a flavour that lingers on the tongue.
—Rosie's Diary

IT WAS a gesture of such intimacy that for a moment Elle couldn't think, couldn't breathe. Rooted to the spot, the only movement was the pulse beating in her neck, the rush of something irresistible sweeping through her veins. A weakness in her legs. The aching pull of desire for something that was unknown and yet as familiar as breathing.

As she swayed towards him, drawn like a magnet towards him, Sean let her hair fall. 'Come on,' he said, moving to the front of the van. 'I'll introduce you to Rosie.'

Elle remained where she was, her skin tingling where the back of his fingers had brushed her cheek. And not just on her cheek. Her entire body felt as if it had been switched on and was fizzing with energy.

'Elle,' Sean said with mock formality, 'may I present Rosie? Rosie, this is Elle. She's Basil's great-niece and your new keeper.'

'Sean,' she protested.

'It's you or Granny,' he reminded her.

'That's playing dirty.' She might have already made up her mind to do the Saturday gig at Longbourne Court, give something back to the Pink Ribbon Club, but that was going to be *the* extent of her involvement. Absolutely. Definitely.

'One of you is the registered keeper,' he pointed out. 'Your choice.'

She glared at him, but at least she was back in control of her legs and she was working on her breathing. 'I've got nowhere to keep her,' she pointed out.

'Won't she go in the garage?'

'The generations of junk only leave room for the car and I can't afford to have that towed to the scrapyard,' she told him.

'I'll do that for you,' he said.

'Oh…' She swallowed. Considering the money they'd spent at the garage over the years, they could have offered to do that for them, but she wouldn't ask. It took a stranger to finally offer his help.

A stranger with an agenda, she reminded herself.

'Any more objections?'

There had to be dozens, but right now she couldn't think of a single one and she turned to the van. 'Okay, Rosie,' she said, 'it seems that whether I like it or not I'm all you've got for now, so here's the way it is. Behave yourself or you'll join the rest of our transport. In the scrapyard.'

'A word of advice, Elle,' Sean said. 'Like most females, Rosie usually responds better to gentle handling.'

Something she was sure he knew from personal experience and she kicked one of the white-walled tyres.

He tutted. 'Asking for trouble,' he said with an annoying you-have-been-warned shake of the head that made her want to kick Rosie again.

'I don't need to ask; it comes calling.' Blue-eyed trouble wearing painted-on jeans and a melt-your-bones smile. 'This time driving a pink van,' she added pointedly.

'Trouble is my middle name,' he admitted. 'So? What do you think of her?'

'Honestly?'

'It's usually best, I find.'

'Yes.'

For a moment their eyes locked, her mouth dried and she turned abruptly to Rosie, staring at her with unseeing eyes while she counted her breath—in one-two-three, out one-two-three—until she was capable of rational thought.

'Honestly…' she repeated as she took in the gentle rounded lines. Honestly, she thought that Rosie looked like something out of a children's story book.

Pink and white with a chrome grille and little round head-lamps that gave the impression of a smiley face. The ice cream cones on either side of the roof, like a pair of rabbit ears, added to the illusion.

The Happy Little Ice Cream Van…

Here Comes the Ice Cream Van…

Jingle Goes the Ice Cream Van…

'I think she's very…shiny,' she said before she completely lost it. Rosie had been polished to a gleaming shine and, despite her advanced age, there was not a sign of rust to mar her im-maculate paintwork. Her hair swung over her face as she bent to take a closer look and she tucked it behind her ear. 'Tell me, did you buff her up specially before you came here?' she asked. 'To make her look particularly appealing?'

'I gave her a once-over with the hose and leather to remove the dust,' he admitted, 'but that's all. Basil wields the wax.'

'Something else he expects me to do, no doubt.'

'I think he'd excuse you the waxing, although no one wants an ice cream from a grubby van.'

'I think, whoever he is, he's got more neck than a giraffe,' she retaliated, taking another walk around her.

She wasn't particularly interested in the quality of Rosie's bodywork, but it was a lot easier to concentrate on the problem with Rosie between them. So that she couldn't see his shoulders, his muscular arms, be sandbagged by those blue eyes.

She paused, let her hand rest against the pink, sun-warmed metal of the door for a moment, trying to connect with this unknown great-uncle who had lavished such love on an inanimate object when he had a family living so close by.

Sean joined her. 'Honestly?' he prompted.

'Honestly, I have to admit that she is rather sweet.'

Okay. She was kidding herself. Her concentration was totally shot.

'Do you want to see inside?'

He didn't wait for an answer, but opened the door and stood back and, as Elle stepped up into the serving area, she was instantly assailed by the faint scent of vanilla, the ghost of untold numbers of ices served in Rosie's long lifetime. Echoes of the excited voices of children.

Her own memories of standing with a coin growing hot in her hand as she'd lined up with her mother to buy an ice at the fair. Not from Rosie… The van had been blue, like the sky, and she'd been happy.

Her heart picked up a beat and her mouth smiled all by itself, no effort involved. Fun. The word popped into her head unbidden. This could be fun.

Danger…

It was as if the word *fun* had clanged a warning in her brain. It couldn't be that simple. There was always a catch. Fun had to be paid for.

And with the thought came a brown envelope dose of reality.

On her hands and knees, scrubbing the kitchen floor, she might bear a passing resemblance to Cinderella but, while Basil fitted the role of Baron Hardup and Sean McElroy was undoubtedly a charmer, this was no fairy tale.

'Will you tell me one thing, Sean?' She looked back over her shoulder. 'Exactly how much rent does Basil owe the estate?'

She hadn't been conscious of him smiling until he stopped but at least he didn't pretend not to know what she was talking about.

'You really think I'd put you out to work to pay off Basil's debts?' he asked, his voice perfectly even.

'Man cannot live by ice cream alone and you seem very eager to drum up business,' she pointed out.

For a heartbeat, the blink of an eye, nothing happened. Then Sean's face emptied of expression.

'I'm convinced, Elle. You don't know Basil. And you certainly don't know me. Step down,' he said, moving back to give her room. She didn't move. 'Step down,' he repeated. 'Walk away and we'll forget this ever happened.'

'Just like that?' When he'd gone out of his way to persuade her that she was responsible? 'What happened to your determination to carry out Basil's wishes, even if it meant bothering a confused old lady?'

She wanted him to tell her that he would never have done that. Instead, he said, 'I'll tell Basil the truth. That you weren't interested.'

'And if he doesn't come back?'

'If he doesn't come back it won't matter one way or the other, will it?'

And, in a heartbeat, the connection between them—sizzling, flashing like that dodgy plug ever since she'd opened the front door and seen him standing on the doorstep—overloaded, snapped. Confused, disorientated, Elle felt as if some internal power switch had tripped out and she'd lost her bearings. Momentarily blind. Adrift. In the dark.

Sean McElroy hadn't raged at her for impugning Basil's character—if a gambler who ran away from his problems leaving someone else to pick up the pieces could be said to possess one. Or, worse, for impugning his own.

He hadn't lost his temper or raised his voice. He had simply switched off. Cut the connection.

She did it herself, using a polite mask to keep the Mrs Fishers of this world at bay, but this was something quite different. She had never dropped her guard with anyone before. Not even her immediate family. But her defences had crumbled beneath the spell of Sean's blue eyes.

She'd never understood why her mother had fallen for the

same line over and over. Now she knew how; lost in the grip of a response so powerful that it overrode sense, you could forget everything. To have that withdrawn was like having the rug pulled out from beneath you.

How could a man with such an expressive face, whose smile lit up a room, blank off his emotions so completely? More to the point, why had he needed to learn?

As always, there were more questions than answers. Only one thing was certain. She'd finally woken up sufficiently to question his motives and, having done so, she'd got exactly what she wanted.

Had wanted.

Life would be a whole lot simpler if she stepped away from Rosie, forgot she'd ever heard the name Basil and let Sean drive away, out of her life, so that she could go back to worrying about tedious stuff like paying the bills. Finding the money for Geli's school trip. Coping with her grandmother's total inability to deal with reality.

A lot safer if she could forget the way her pulse had quickened at the touch of his hand on her shoulder, her cheek, her hair. If she could tell him to walk away and leave Rosie to her. That she'd cope without him.

If only it were that simple. The Pink Ribbon Club was relying on Rosie to turn up next Saturday and she was determined to fulfil that obligation. Not just for the PRC but for herself. Stepping outside her small world and doing something positive, meaningful would give her a sense of accomplishment, self-worth.

Which left the small matter of the ice cream machine. While she might be able to work it out for herself, she could just as easily mess it up.

One look at his face, however, warned her that it was going to take a lot more than a simple, *I'm sorry, my mistake* to switch Sean McElroy back on. Soften eyes that were now the blue of case-hardened steel. Tease out the melt-your-bones smile that had been wiped from his face as cleanly as the incoming tide washed lines from the sand.

She took a deep breath. Okay. She'd been dealing with difficult situations since she was a teenager, confronting adults who thought they were dealing with a child. In a situation like that you learned fast not to show weakness, fear.

And, despite his annoyance, she had every right to question what he was getting out of this. He'd dumped and run yesterday, offloading Rosie without a second thought. So why had he come back?

Her hormones might be drowning in drool, but she doubted it was her sex appeal that was the draw. After all, he'd had the possessively glamorous blonde more than willing to keep him warm last night.

'You're right, Sean. I don't know Basil. By his choice,' she reminded him. 'And, right again, I don't know a thing about you either, but that's a two-way deal.' She didn't wait for his reaction, but took a step further into the van, ran her hand over the serving counter, slid back the window, making it her own before she glanced back at him. 'Neither of you knows a thing about me.'

She'd banked on him following her. He didn't fall for it. Didn't move, didn't speak. Simply waited for her to take a look around and then step out again so that he could drive away. And why wouldn't he? She was the one who'd been vehemently insisting that she didn't want to know.

It wasn't true, she discovered.

She wanted to know everything. Wanted to know about her mysterious great-uncle. Wanted to know what her grandmother had done for him. Why he'd been wiped from the family memory. Where he'd been all these years. Wanted to know what made Sean McElroy tick.

No. Scrub that last one.

She examined the stacked up cartons containing cones and the plastic shells used to serve ice cream sundaes.

'Did Basil usually leave all these inside the van?' she asked. Sean didn't answer. She turned to look at him.

'I have no idea,' he finally answered.

'His letter suggests he always intended to send Rosie here.' She shifted the boxes of cones to uncover pallets containing litre cartons of UHT ice cream mix. She poked a hole in the shrink-wrap and removed one to take a closer look. 'You did assume we were expecting her. A mistake anyone might make under the circumstances,' she added mildly, looking down at him through the open window. And prompted a slight frown to add to the tightened jaw.

Content that she'd re-established a connection, even if it was at the frowning end of the spectrum, Elle set the carton down on the serving shelf, leaving him to contemplate the fact that he wasn't infallible while she explored the storage cupboards.

'Generations of my family have lived in Gable End,' she said conversationally, filling the knowledge gap, then blinked at the powerful hit of chocolate as she lifted the lid on a box of flakes. 'Basil must have grown up here.'

She took one, bit into it. Used a finger to catch a crumb of chocolate on her lip, sucked it.

'My great-grandfather, Bernard's father and apparently Basil's too, was a stockbroker,' she went on, continuing to explore the contents of the cupboard. 'Did Basil tell you that?'

'We confined our conversation to the state of Rosie's working parts.'

Mini marshmallows, nuts…

Elle had a distant memory of an ice cream studded with marshmallows, her mother's laughter…

'He was a magistrate, too,' she said. 'And a parish councillor. A pillar of the community.'

'Stiff collar, stiff manners and a stiff upper lip,' he commented with perfect understanding.

Finally, a response to something other than a direct question. 'I couldn't say. I never knew him.' Then, frowning, she looked up from a box of multicoloured sprinkles. 'Do you have a problem with respectability?'

His response was the slowest of shrugs. She waited and, finally, he said, 'It's nothing but a façade constructed to cover a multitude of sins.'

'You really think that?' she asked, jerked out of her carefully orchestrated build-up of family history to justify her trust issues. Not that they needed justifying, she reminded herself. She had a family to protect and had every right to be cautious.

'I wouldn't say it if I didn't know it to be true,' he said.

'Strange. While you lack the collar, you've got the stiffest lip, the stiffest neck I've ever encountered.'

That caught him off guard. Surprised him. His recovery was swift but she'd cracked the mask.

'Maybe I have a problem with narrow-minded people who see anyone who isn't like them as a threat,' he said. 'Who look the part but don't live it.'

Oh, now that was telling. Did he see himself as an outsider? Why?

'I can go along with that,' she said carefully, 'but certain rules are made for the common good. There are some things you can't take on trust.' She thumbed an imaginary smear off the hygiene certificate fixed to the interior of the van. 'Even Basil understood that.' Then, turning back to the carton of ice cream mix, 'I wonder if they do this in strawberry.'

She knew he was watching her, eyes narrowed, not sure what she was up to. That made two of them. Her common sense genes, the ones she'd inherited from the magistrate, and from Grandpa, were urging her to let it go. Let him go.

But suddenly she wasn't so sure about those respectable citizens any more. The ones she had worked so hard to emulate.

What kind of people cut off a member of their family? Wiped him out of existence?

'Sean?' she prompted, refusing to be ignored.

'Yes, strawberry and chocolate too,' he told her. Voice clipped, determined not to be drawn in.

'But not everyone likes strawberry ice cream, do they?' She raised an eyebrow, inviting his opinion, then, when he didn't offer one, 'Perhaps it would be safer to simply add a few drops of cochineal to the vanilla.'

'Cochineal?'

'It's a natural food colouring. Made from crushed beetles.'

'What are you talking about?'

She didn't rush to answer but put the carton down and turned her attention to the machine, lifting the lid to peer inside, letting her fingers play over the controls.

He said nothing.

She pulled on a lever.

'Lovage Amery,' he warned.

'La, la, la…' she sang, just like her grandmother when she was pretending not to hear. And laughed as, just like that, she discovered how her grandmother had got her nickname.

Sean swore under his breath as he stepped up, grabbed her wrist before she did any damage.

But that was the point of the exercise. To get him inside the van with her. Listening to her. Talking to her.

He'd watched her exploring the interior of the van, reeling him in with her mindless chatter and her come-and-stop-me-if-you-dare exploration of the machinery.

He'd been taken in by the blush, but while she might, impossibly for a grown woman, seem much too innocent for that luscious mouth and gorgeous body, she was nobody's fool.

It had finally occurred to her to challenge Basil's motives in asking for her help. Or, rather, her grandmother's help. Fair enough. He'd be asking questions if some stranger pitched up on his doorstep selling him a story about a long lost relative, burdening him with a high maintenance vehicle and a lot of hard work for little or no reward. Looking for the catch.

But he didn't care what she thought about Basil. Elle had changed *his* motives, *his* probity and, even after all these years, it was like being back in school, taunted with his background. Not one of *us*. Not in the local primary school where his father's title had been the barrier. Not at the expensive boarding school either, where his mother had been the problem. A cold draught on the exposed nerve of tooth.

'Crushed beetles?' he asked as she turned to him, her face all did-I-do-something-wrong? innocent.

Her eyes betrayed her. They glinted with something that matched the unconscious sex appeal. Threw out a reckless challenge that suggested there was someone else hidden inside her head, someone entirely different to the face she showed the world. Which of them, he wondered, would turn up if he did what he'd been thinking about ever since she'd opened the front door yesterday afternoon? If he put his arms around her and kissed her? The outraged innocent? Or the woman he'd glimpsed behind those eyes?

'It's pink food colouring,' she said. 'Completely natural. No E numbers. Pink ices for the Pink Ribbon Club?' she said. 'What do you think?'

He was thinking about her breath against his mouth, the softness of her skin, his fingers sliding through that silky mane of hair...

There were tiny florets of lilac caught up in it, he noticed. He'd watched her from the window as she'd buried her head in the bush and the scent of the flowers mingled with warm skin and the herby tang of shampoo. He wanted to lay his face against her neck and breathe it in.

'I think you'd have to label it unsuitable for vegetarians,' he said, keeping his eyes fixed on the food hygiene certificate. Rules... He had rules about sticking to women who understood that he didn't do emotional attachment. Commitment. Who just wanted to have fun.

'Good point. Pink sprinkles, then?' Her face relaxed into the smile she'd been fighting, lifting the corners of her mouth in careless enticement.

In his head he had rules, but his body was responding on instinct, urging him to make a move. Telling him that she wanted it as much as he did. That if he kissed her it wouldn't just make *his* day. It would make hers, too.

'Pink sprinkles it is,' he managed, hanging onto his concentration by his fingernails. Keeping his eyes level with the top of her head.

That was when he saw the ladybird taking a precipitous walk along a silky strand, the perfect distraction until it slipped and fell, tiny legs waving, no doubt wondering what the heck had just happened.

'Wouldn't it be perfect if you could buy pink chocolate flakes?' she said.

One minute you were minding your own business, quietly milking the greenfly and the next, wham, you were in the dark, your world turned upside down.

Pretty much the way Elle must be feeling right now. Although he was beginning to suspect that her world hadn't been that great to begin with.

'You can get white ones so pink shouldn't be such a stretch. Sean?' she prompted.

'Hold still,' he said, releasing her hand so that he could gently part her hair to set the ladybird free to fly away.

Her forehead puckered in a frown. 'What are you doing?'

'Extracting a real live beetle. If you will stick your head in a bush you must expect to attract the local wildlife.'

It was her cue to squeal. Fling herself into his arms. All she said was, 'Don't hurt it.'

'I'm doing my best, but it's all tangled up. You'll have to come closer.'

'Is it all right?' she asked anxiously, leaning into him.

'Give me a minute,' he muttered. More than a minute because, while she was showing no sign of girly nerves, both he and the ladybird were in a whole heap of trouble.

The bug, being a bug, didn't know it had to follow Elle's example of zen-like calm, keep still and co-operate. Instead, it panicked, getting into deeper trouble as it tried to right itself.

And Sean's hands were beginning to shake so badly that he was only making things worse.

'You were telling me your family history,' he said in an effort to distract himself from the warmth of her breath against his chest. Her breast nestling against his arm. 'Your grandfather,' he prompted. 'Bernard inherited the house?'

'As far as I know.' She looked up. 'The official version of family history is that he was an only child. Did he buy his brother out? I wonder. Or was Basil cut out of the will.' She was shaken by an involuntary shiver that telegraphed itself through his body. Elle was clearly a lot more upset at the discovery that her respectable elders weren't quite what they seemed than she was prepared to say. At least he'd had no illusions to shatter. 'How are you doing?' she asked.

'Can you move a little to the right?' he requested, his voice emerging through cobwebs that seemed to be blocking his throat.

'I barely knew him. My grandfather,' she added as she shifted a little, leaning closer so that more of her was in contact with more of him. 'He wasn't the kind of grandpa who sat you on his knee and read to you. Played Happy Families on a wet Sunday afternoon. I don't think he was a happy man.'

'Maybe he had a guilty conscience,' he suggested.

'Maybe. Would this be easier if we went outside?'

'Just keep still,' he said, putting his arm around her to keep her from moving away just as the ladybird finally got with the plot and crawled onto his finger. 'What happened when he died?'

'Nothing much. He left us all pretty well provided for and being a single mother wasn't that big a deal by then. Although three different fathers did tend to raise eyebrows.'

'Three?'

'I told you,' she said. 'History. We don't look a bit alike. Sorrel has red hair and under the black dye Geli is white blonde.'

While her hair was the colour and shine of the chocolate sauce Basil used on his ices.

'It must have been hard when she died,' he said. 'Your mother.'

'It knocked us all sideways for a long time, but then Gran met someone. Andrew. At least that's what he said his name was. He was charming, well-mannered and he made the world seem a brighter place for a while. It felt like we'd turned a corner. I'd scraped through my exams and had a place in the local college, a future, plans...'

She stopped, taking a moment to gather herself.

'It was all a con, of course.'

Of course.

'He parted Gran from her cash with the ease of a fishmonger filleting a trout, promising her the kind of interest rates that disappeared a decade ago. All very hush-hush, naturally. She was one of the lucky ones but she had to keep it to herself or everyone would pile in. Spoil it.'

'And once he had it all, he disappeared,' Sean finished for her.

At some point during the wind up of her story, the point she'd been trying to make about why she couldn't just trust him, his other arm had found its way around her so that he was holding her close.

'She must have realised pretty quickly, but the first I knew about the whole sorry mess was when I opened the door to a strange man who asked if I was Lovage Amery.' She pulled back her head, looked up into his face. 'I said yes, just as I did to you yesterday, and found myself holding a brown envelope.'

Sean remembered the way she'd avoided taking the one he'd been holding. Putting her hands behind her back.

'Was it a summons?'

'The first of many. Gran had been hiding the final demands from the utilities, the credit card companies, most for cards he'd applied for using her name...'

He muttered something under his breath as he realised what had happened.

'...and of course the letters from the bank. He did a pretty good job of forging her signature to clear out everything she hadn't already handed over. She'd been hoping against hope he'd come back before she had to face up to the truth.'

'At least you managed to hang onto the house,' he said helplessly.

'Only because Grandpa left it in trust for his grandchildren, so it wasn't hers to lose. Gran has the use of it for her lifetime but even if she died it can't be sold until the youngest of us is twenty-one. That's Geli. She's sixteen,' she added, almost as if she was warning him that there was no hope of money coming from that direction—and who could blame her? 'He never knew her, of course. Mum was still expecting Sorrel when he died. But maybe he understood Gran a lot better than we did.'

CHAPTER SIX

Everyone has a price. Mine is ice cream.
                                        —Rosie's Diary

'You take after your grandfather.'

'Do I?' Elle pulled a face. 'I'm sure you mean that kindly, but if you'd known him you'd understand that's not a compliment.'

'I just meant that you're the responsible one. The one who worries about money. Takes care of everything. Everyone.'

Elle closed her eyes, remembering the embarrassment of the bailiff removing paintings, Great-Grandma's jewellery—Andrew had packed her grandmother's jewellery in his overnight case when he'd left 'for a business meeting'. The wedding china, family silver, antique furniture had all gone. Anything that would raise hard cash until all the debts had been paid.

They were fortunate there had been so much, but it hadn't felt like it at the time. When everyone stopped talking as she walked into the village shop each Monday morning to collect the child allowance from the post office after Gran had taken to her bed. Sticking her fingers in her ears, figuratively speaking, and la-la-ing until it had all gone away.

It had been the only cash coming in until she'd surrendered her place in college for a minimum wage job at the Blue Boar. Cleaning, working in the kitchen, before Freddy had moved her into the restaurant.

It had been the only job within walking distance from home. They hadn't been able to afford bus fares or petrol for the car and she had to be near enough to get home if her grandmother needed her.

She knew now that Social Services would have helped but at the time she'd been so afraid that, with her grandmother turning her face to the wall, they would have taken Sorrel and Geli into care if she'd asked for help.

'Responsibility wasn't a choice, Sean.'

'No.' Then, again, 'No. Look, don't bother your head about all this,' he said, holding her close. 'I'll keep Rosie until Basil turns up. And I'll take care of Saturday too.'

'So…what?' She leaned back to look him full in the face, her hands on his chest. 'Are you saying that you don't need me after all?'

Oh, no, he wasn't saying that. Holding her this way was stirring up the kind of basic need that had nothing to do with serving ice cream and if he didn't let her go, right now, she'd know it too.

The difference being that he understood that it was no more than a temporary, self-serving need. Nothing more than a passing attraction. He only did 'passing'; he had no understanding of any other kind of relationship.

Even while his body was demanding he go for it, his head knew that she wasn't kind of girl to indulge in a light-hearted, no-strings, bed-and-breakfast flirtation; the kind a man could walk away from with a clear conscience.

Elle had suffered enough hurt in her short life and while she would, inevitably, get her heart broken sooner or later, he would not be the one responsible for that.

'It's Basil who needs you,' he said, mentally distancing himself from her. 'But you're right, why should you put yourself out for a man you don't know, have never met? Who has never done a thing for you?'

'It's a mystery,' she said. 'As inexplicable as why he came to us for help after forty years of silence. Any ideas about that?'

'None whatever,' he said. 'But then family is not my special-ist subject.'

'Mine either, it would seem. But I do know that what you have you should hold on to. Love them, keep them safe, what-ever they do.'

And there it was. Right there. The reason he needed to step away. If he hadn't recognised her vulnerability within minutes of setting eyes on her, her belief in the importance of family, all the things he despised, would have sent up the kind of warning flares that a man who believed in nothing, no one, would do well to heed.

'Like your grandfather. Like you,' he said.

Take your hands off her now, McElroy.

'Maybe. How's the ladybird doing?' she asked.

'She gave up on me and rescued herself some time ago,' he admitted.

Step back…

'Did she?' She smiled. 'Well, good for her. She did a good job holding your attention while I explained why I have trust issues.'

'You had me at crushed beetles,' he admitted.

She smiled. 'I knew that would do it.'

Let her go…

'Actually,' he said, 'I think you're right about that. I'll stick with the pink sprinkles.'

'What makes you think you've got a say in the matter?' she asked. 'Rosie is mine, remember? It's my name on the logbook.'

'Are you telling me that you're going to keep her?'

'*You* had *me* at the Pink Ribbon Club, Sean. Just for Saturday. Lavender's girls have a debt to pay them. All I need from you is a quick tutorial.'

That wicked little come-and-get-me glint was back in her eyes now that she'd broken down the barrier he'd instinc-tively thrown up. It was the look of a woman who had won hands down and left him out for the count. But the bell hadn't rung yet.

His legs had ignored him, his hands were still resting just below her shoulder blades keeping her close, his thighs against her hips, and this time he'd didn't waste time asking himself which woman would show up if he kissed her.

He had to know.

Her eyes widened slightly as his mouth slowly descended, giving her all the time in the world to say no, do what he'd be unable to do and step back.

Her lips did part, as if she might say something, but all that emerged was a little quiver of breath, warm, faintly chocolatey, mingling with his own. Fizzing through his blood, intoxicating as vintage champagne, and he was within a hair's breadth of going to hell in a handcart when a crunch on the gravel, a loud, 'It's still here!' warned them that they were no longer alone.

'Geli…'

The blush was in full working order and he didn't need to send frantic instructions to his legs to move before he did something stupid. Elle did it for him, springing back as if she'd been caught with her hand in the till.

'I wasn't expecting you back so soon,' she said to her sister.

'Obviously.'

Sarcasm as only a teenager could do it.

Elle shut the serving window, not looking at Sean as she jumped down, her wobbly legs buckling as she hit the gravel in her eagerness to put some distance between herself and temptation.

As she put some stiffeners into her knees, she couldn't decide whether she was furious with her sister for turning up just as she was about to taste heaven, or grateful that she'd been saved from the biggest mistake in her life.

A quick tutorial…

What had she been thinking?

Thinking? That was joke.

For a moment back there it had been the gallopers, the waltzer, the big wheel, all the fun of the fair rolled into one and she'd been gone, with only one thought in her head. The one that confirmed she was her mother's daughter.

Wham, bang, thank you, ma'am.

'So are you going to tell me why we have an ice cream van parked in the drive?' Geli demanded.

Her youngest sister was definitely *not* going to be impressed by anything so defiantly pink and white invading her space. And, having glared at Rosie, she turned her attention to Sean.

'And who *is* he?'

Beneath the aggression, Elle recognised fear. Geli's body was maturing but, despite the emerging curves, she was still a child who'd never had a father and had lost her mother at a tragically early age.

Before she could reassure her, Sorrel walked through the gate, their grandmother at her side.

For a moment Elle held her breath, but her grandmother just smiled. 'Are we going to have ice cream?' she asked. 'How lovely. Can I have chocolate sauce?'

Sean glanced at her, clearly surprised that her grandmother hadn't recognised him, unfamiliar with Lally's ability to completely block out anything she didn't want to remember.

'Not just now, Gran. Sean is busy and I have to go to work.'

'Sean?'

'Sean McElroy,' he said, going with it and introducing himself before turning to her sisters. 'And you must be Sorrel?'

Sorrel threw Elle an amused look of approval. 'I'm Sorrel Amery, and this is Geli,' she said, hand outstretched. Despite being five years younger than Elle, Sorrel had the galling ability to appear the most adult of all of them. She was taking a degree in business studies and it was her stated intention to be a millionaire by the time she was twenty-five. She already acted and dressed the part.

Geli glared at Sorrel. 'My name is Angelica,' she said, which wasn't promising. She only ever used her full name when she was in the kind of mood that meant trouble. 'And we've already met.'

'How was church this morning?' Elle asked quickly before this conversation could develop into something her grandmother couldn't deal with.

'Oh, the sermon just went on and on so I left the vicar to it and went to find Sorrel,' Gran said.

'But she was supposed to be working!' Elle tried not to sound as exasperated as she felt. Freddy had given Sorrel permission to use the free Wi-Fi provided for the bed and breakfast businessmen but only at the weekend when they weren't busy. He certainly wouldn't appreciate her family turning up en masse.

'I didn't get in her way. I just sat and read all the lovely free newspapers in the lounge while she downloaded stuff from the Internet.'

Elle groaned. 'You'll get me the sack.'

'Oh, please.' Sorrel rolled her eyes. 'Freddy is never going to fire you; he's too desperate to get into your knickers.'

'No, no, no!' Geli declared, covering her ears with her hands. 'I'm too young to have that picture in my head.'

'Quite right, Geli. Don't be vulgar, Sorrel.' Gran patted her hair. 'Mr Frederickson was very kind. He brought us coffee and muffins and stayed to chat with me while Sorrel was busy. He's very fond of you, Elle.'

Geli snorted.

'He appreciates how hard you work, and wants to promote you to assistant manager,' Gran told her gleefully.

'I know, but I can't take the job.' A promotion would mean long hours with no chance to switch and swap shifts. And while the money would be more, she'd lose her tips. 'Now, if he offered me an extra fifty pence an hour,' she said, determined to turn the conversation away from any interest Freddy had in her knickers. Like Geli, the image was not something she wanted in her head. 'Well, that would be very welcome.'

'No such luck,' Sorrel said. 'He was just trying to make me feel guilty before he offered me a job.'

He certainly hadn't wasted any time. 'You don't need a job. I want you to stick to your college work so that you can keep me in my old age,' Elle said lightly.

'No nuts with the ice cream, young man,' her grandmother said, so quickly that if Elle didn't know better she might have imagined Gran was feeling guilty about Elle's lost opportunities. Then, taking Sorrel's arm, 'Let's go and have another cup of coffee. Elle never makes any these days. I'd forgotten how much I enjoyed it.'

Unfortunately, Geli didn't follow them.

'You know that Freddy was just plying Gran with coffee and cake so that he could pump her about what you do in your spare time?'

'Geli—'

'He wants to be sure you aren't spending it with some fit bloke. If he hears that you've been flirting with the ice cream man,' she said, giving Sean a flint-eyed stare, 'you can kiss your job goodbye.'

'Don't be silly,' Elle said uncomfortably, unwilling to get into any conversation that involved the word kissing—not when she could almost taste Sean on her lips. 'I thought you were meeting up with some friends from school and going into Maybridge this morning,' she said, dragging her mind back to reality.

'They decided to go to the multiplex in Melchester. Apparently, they've opened a new burger bar. Yuck, yuck, yuck.'

'Geli…Angelica…is a vegetarian.' Elle finally risked a glance at Sean.

'Really? It's a good thing you abandoned the crushed beetles option, then,' he said, his face perfectly straight.

Geli looked at him, looked at her, then said, 'Too weird. I'm going to get something to eat.'

'Geli—'

'What!'

'There's no milk,' Elle reminded her.

'Don't blame me!'

'Or bread.'

She sighed dramatically, then flounced off towards the village.

'Is it always like this?' Sean asked.

'Just an average day at Gable End.' Apart from Rosie. Long lost uncles. And a kiss that was no more than a breath on her lips.

'I'd better go,' Sean said. 'I've already got you into enough trouble without making you late for work.'

'Don't take any notice of Geli. I've worked for Freddy for seven years.'

'He's a patient man.'

'Patient?'

'Although you would have been rather young for him when you first started. What is he? Forty? Forty-five?'

Her cheeks heated up as she realised what he meant. 'No, Freddy's not interested in me in that way. It's just Sorrel's idea of a joke.'

His eyebrows barely moved. 'If you say so,' he said, looking not at her, but at Rosie. 'I never did get around to showing you how the ice cream machine works.'

Maybe not, but he'd come very close to showing her plenty of other things. With her whole-hearted co-operation.

Not that he seemed in any great hurry to resume the lesson where they'd left off—touching close, lips a murmur apart. And that was a Good Thing, she told herself.

She might not have entirely escaped her mother's live-now pay-later nature, but that didn't mean she had to follow her example and lose her head over the first man to make her heart, and just about everything else, go boom.

'There's no time now. Save it for Saturday,' she said.

'Saturday?'

'I'm sorry,' she said, arranging her face in a faintly puzzled frown, 'but didn't you volunteer to be in charge of the sprinkles?'

'Did I?' And there it was again. The barely-there smile that went straight to her knees.

'And afterwards you can take Rosie back to Haughton Manor and tuck her up in your barn until Basil turns up,' she added, making an effort to be sensible.

Something else he'd volunteered to do before they'd both forgotten about Rosie, ice cream, Basil...

'Oh, no! The letter!'

Sean should have been feeling only one emotion as he watched Elle race back down the path, long legs, long hair flying, to retrieve Basil's letter before her grandmother picked it up and read it.

Relief.

He'd come within a gnat's whisker of losing control, but Elle had just given him a get-out-of-jail-free card and it was long past time to remove himself from the temptation of those luscious lips, the danger of entanglement in a situation that should have a dedicated commitment-phobe running a mile.

'Saturday it is, then,' he said to no one in particular as he shut Rosie's door, locked up, gave her a little pat. 'I'll come over early and make sure you behave yourself.'

And he tried not to think about spending an afternoon in close confinement with Elle. The quick tutorial he'd promised her. Or the possessive way the guy who ran the Blue Boar had touched her arm.

Elle skidded to a stop in the doorway. Sorrel was standing by the table reading Basil's letter.

'Where's Gran?' Elle asked.

'Washing her hands. Tidying her hair. Getting ready for that "nice young man with the ice cream",' Sorrel added, patting her hair, mimicking her grandmother perfectly.

'There is no ice cream. At least not today.' She had half

expected Sean to follow her, but she was the one who'd said there was no time. 'Sean's gone.'

'Shame. I hoped you were getting serious attention from someone a little more appealing than Freddy,' her sister teased.

'I've locked up.'

Elle had sensed Sean's presence a fraction of a second before he spoke. A subtle change in the light, the widening in Sorrel's eyes, a charge in the air that had the fine hairs on her skin springing to attention...

Sean put Rosie's keys on the kitchen table. 'I'll come back later with the trailer and pick up the car.'

'Oh, yes. Of course.' She forgotten all about his promise to take their car to the scrapyard. 'I won't be here, but Sorrel...' her beautiful, elegant sister, the one in control of her hair, her figure, her life, if not her tongue '...will be here if you need a hand.'

'If you give me the keys, I won't have to bother anyone,' he said.

'Of course.' Elle took them from the key cupboard and dropped them into his palm, taking care not to touch him. 'I'll leave the garage door unlocked.'

'I'm not sure how much I can get for it,' he warned.

'Get for it? I was told I'd have to pay to have it towed to the scrapyard.'

'When you need towing you're in a buyer's market. I'll take a look at what needs doing, make a few calls. It's possible you'd do better advertising it on the Internet,' he told her.

'I didn't expect you to go to all that trouble,' Elle protested.

'Who'd buy it?' Sorrel asked at the same time.

He looked up. 'You'd be surprised,' he said, answering her sister. Then, in the slightly awkward silence that followed, 'I'll be here at about eleven on Saturday, if that's okay? It should give us plenty of time to run through everything before we go.'

'Thanks.'

'Tell your grandmother she can have all the ice cream she can eat then.'

'She'll enjoy that,' Elle said.

He nodded and was gone.

Elle turned on her sister, hands to her cheeks. 'Did he hear?'

'Does it matter?' she asked.

'"Getting serious attention?" Could you have made me sound more desperate?'

'Elle, you *are* desperate. If you're not careful, you'll succumb to Freddy out of sheer frustration.'

'Don't…' She took a deep breath. 'Just don't…'

'Only saying. You need to grab that one while he's available.'

'He's not,' she said shortly. He might have come close to kissing her just now but he'd been firmly attached to the linen-clad blonde last night. Or she'd been firmly attached to him. Which amounted to the same thing. She should be grateful to Geli for turning up when she had.

Give her a little time and she would be.

'But—'

'The subject is closed,' Elle announced firmly.

'Okay. But you could have cut the tension in here just now with a knife,' Sorrel remarked.

'C-L-O-S-'

'Okay, okay, okay.' Her sister held up the letter. 'Tell me about Basil.'

Grateful for the change of subject, Elle took the letter from her, giving her a quick rundown on the story so far as she folded it up and put it back in the brown envelope, along with the documents and diary.

'I'll do some digging on the 'net. See what I can find out,' Sorrel said, beating her to the top of the range cellphone and switching it on.

'I think you should stay away from the Blue Boar for a while. Freddy wasn't joking about offering you a job,' Elle warned.

'I know. He gave me the whole fitting-around-college-work, great-tips hard sell this morning. I told him I'd think about it. I could do with a new laptop,' she mused.

No...

'I'll see what I can do,' Elle said. Maybe there was something in the attic that had been overlooked. That she could sell. 'Just concentrate on college, get a good degree. When you're a millionaire you can run this family. Meanwhile, will you turn off that phone and give it to me?'

'I'm sorry?'

Not half as sorry as she was, Elle thought, holding out her hand. Sorrel did not hand over the phone. 'What?' Elle asked.

'I'm eighteen, Elle. An adult.'

'You're a student—'

'I'm old enough to vote, fight for my country, buy a bottle of wine and drink it if I want to. I don't want to "run this family", but I will run my own life,' Sorrel insisted.

'How?' Elle demanded. 'You don't even know how to use an iron!'

'It's not rocket science.'

For a moment the room silently vibrated with years of unspoken resentment. Elle's dreams and thwarted ambitions, pushed aside while she stepped up to keep them together. A family.

'No...' Elle took a deep, shuddering breath. 'You don't understand,' she said. 'I just don't want you to be...'

'What? Like you?'

'That would be a woman with no qualifications, no career.' No dream to inspire her. Just living from week to week, from hand to mouth, holding everything together. 'Point made, I think.'

'Elle...' Sorrel shook her head. 'I could never be you. You saved us from being put into care, saved Gran from completely losing her marbles. But maybe it's time to think about saving yourself now.'

'I don't need saving,' she insisted. Perhaps a little bit too fiercely, too defensively. 'But I'll think about it. If you'll forget about working at the Blue Boar.'

'Oh, please. If I want a job, I can do better than skivvying for Freddy.' Elle was still struggling to catch her breath when she added, 'In fact, with a phone like this, I'd never have to go near the place again. And you read Basil's letter. He's handed everything over to us. Asked us to take care of things'

'Sorrel…'

'He's got messages. Mostly people asking him to give them a ring,' she said, flicking through them. 'You can't ignore them.'

'Can't I?' Elle said dryly.

'Oh, no, this is different. "Change in schedule."' she read. '"Need van on Tuesday. Upper Haughton location. Eight a.m. Confirm. KS."' She looked up. 'What do you think that means?'

'I've no idea.'

'I could call him and find out?' she offered.

'If you want to be useful, Sorrel,' Elle snapped, taking the phone out of her hand and switching it off, 'prove how adult you are, you can start by organising some lunch for Geli and Gran.'

Sean wasted no time going back with the trailer to pick up Elle's old crock while she was at work.

Geli came out, standing pointedly, arms crossed, keeping an eye on him. A couple of neighbours walked slowly past, lingering by the gate. He kept his head down, his mouth shut and wished he'd waited until later. When Elle was home.

What better way to spend a Sunday afternoon than making ice cream? Maybe he could have persuaded her to take a walk by the river. They could have had a drink at the pub down by the lock. They might even have finished that kiss…

'Do you want me to drive Rosie into the garage?' he asked Geli.

'Did Elle ask you to?'

'No.'

She shrugged, walked away.

He took a deep breath and told himself that Saturday was quite soon enough.

CHAPTER SEVEN

If your ice cream melts, you're eating it too slowly.
—Rosie's Diary

ELLE found Monday a mixed sort of day. It was her day off, which meant she didn't have to be on her feet for hours, a smile on her face no matter what.

On the downside, it was the day she tackled the business end of life. Paid bills. Dealt with 'stuff'. She didn't enjoy it but, having lived with the results of her grandmother sticking her head in the sand and not dealing with it, she never put it off.

First thing every Monday morning, she holed up in the little office she'd made for herself in a bedroom which, back in the days when the Amery name was respected, had been the quarters of a live-in maid. At her desk, she could pretend that she was running her own business. Nothing huge. She'd never had her sister's ambition. But doing the accounts, balancing the books, planning menus, shopping lists, she could, for an hour a week, lose herself.

Today, thanks to Great-Uncle Basil, there was more 'stuff' than usual. Messages to deal with. Appointments to cancel. No time for dreaming.

Having balanced the weekly accounts, checking every detail to make sure that nothing had been overlooked, she picked up the bells-and-whistles phone that had caught Sorrel's eye, turned it on and started with the most urgent of the messages.

'Basil?' a hard male voice snapped before she could speak. 'Where have you been?'

'Actually, I'm not Basil,' Elle said. 'My name is Lovage Amery…' it had to be the first time she'd voluntarily used the name but it had a rather more authoritative ring to it than Elle '…and I'm responding to a message left on his phone. Who am I speaking to?'

Always get a name. Make a note of any phone call. Confirm the relevant points in writing. Hard-learned lessons.

'Sutherland. Sutherland Productions,' he said impatiently. She wrote it down. 'Tell Basil I need the van in Upper Haughton at eight o'clock on Tuesday morning. We've got to shoot these outdoor scenes while the weather holds.'

Scenes?

'I'm sorry, Mr Sutherland. Basil has been called away and he won't be available—'

'What do you mean, called away? Who are you?'

'Lovage Amery,' she repeated.

'You're what? His wife, daughter?'

'Niece.' Allegedly.

'Well, Lovage, here's the bottom line. Your uncle signed a contract with my production company. What's more, he took a deposit.'

Her heart missed a beat. 'But he's not here,' she said, doing her best to keep calm. 'He's away on business.'

'Did he take the van with him?'

'Well, no—'

'Then what's the problem? The contract's for the van, a driver and a full load of ice cream. Just make sure it's in Upper Haughton at eight o'clock tomorrow morning.'

'But you don't understand—'

'No, love, *you* don't understand. If the van's not there, on time, ready to go on Tuesday morning, he's going to be responsible for all costs involved in finding a replacement.'

Elle felt the bottom fall out of her stomach. 'Costs?'

'The film crew, the actors on standby and if I lose the weather—'

Actors? What on earth had Basil got her into?

'That won't be necessary,' she said quickly. 'I'll be there.'

'Don't be late.'

'Can you tell me how long it's likely to take?' she said quickly before he hung up.

'I've booked the van for the whole day, but an hour should do it, love,' he said, and then she was listening to the dialling tone.

Elle put down the phone and said, '*Lovage*. It's *Lovage*.' Then she tucked her hands beneath her arms to stop them shaking.

Her first call and already she was being threatened with the law by some bully of a man Basil had signed a contract with. Taken money from. Who called her 'love'.

And there were dozens of messages...

She made it to the bathroom before she threw up, sank down onto the floor, head on her knees, arms around her legs, shivering.

'Elle...?'

She gathered herself, looked up, saw the fear in her grandmother's eyes.

'It's okay, Gran. Nothing to worry about.'

'Really?'

'Really,' she said, pushing herself to her feet. Her legs still felt wobbly hollow, but she managed a smile. 'Just something I ate. I'm feeling much better now.'

Angry was better than sick. And she was very angry.

Angry with Sean, who'd mesmerised her with those blue eyes. Even when she doubted him, doubted Basil, she'd fallen under his spell.

Angry with herself for bothering to explain her trust issues as if she was in the wrong for doubting him, instead of sticking with her instincts, questioning his motives.

Angry that she'd allowed sentiment to override her natural

caution. Or was it simply lust turning her brain to mush? A genetic flaw...

It took her nearly an hour to return calls, check the diary for the next couple of months. Follow up bookings. And when she was done she had a list of dates, places, names and phone numbers of more than a dozen people who Basil had taken money from. Who expected Rosie to turn up and do her stuff. Seven birthday parties, not all of them for children, a silver wedding anniversary, a hen night, a wedding, a company party, a retirement and the film company.

So much 'fun'.

Not.

Just a logistical nightmare to fit in around her working schedule.

As if that hadn't been enough, the post had brought Rosie's new logbook, proving that this hadn't been a spur of the moment thing.

It would have taken the licensing authority a minimum of a week to turn that around.

Basil had planned this. He'd taken deposits to fund his flight and now either she, or her grandmother, was Rosie's registered keeper. It made no difference. Elle, as always, was the one who'd have to deal with the fallout.

'Thanks! Thanks a bunch!'

Sean was looking at proposals for the new treetop walk laid out on the map table when Elle burst into his office.

Her cheeks were flushed, her hair looked as if she'd been combing it with a pencil—or maybe a pen since she appeared to have a streak of ink at her temple—and her hazel eyes were blazing with golden sparks that lit up his office like the sun coming out on a dull day.

'Lovage...' The name suited her so much better than the bland 'Elle'. Felt so right on his tongue.

A seething little noise escaped her lips. 'Don't you dare "Lovage" me. I am Elle. Elle for livid.'

'I'm sorry, Sean.' Jess, the estate secretary, hurried in after her but he shook his head, waved her off. She shrugged and left the room.

The surveyor, avoiding his eyes, rolled up his drawings. 'I'll take a look at this and get back to you later in the week, Sean,' he said, visibly smirking as he shut the door on his way out.

Not surprising. She looked like a brown hen he'd kept as a boy, her feathers ruffled up when the cockerel had taken liberties.

He fought the smile. She was mad enough already.

'Problem?' he asked.

'You could say that. I've got a television producer threatening to sue me if I don't turn up tomorrow on set with a full load of ice cream. Apparently, Basil not only signed a contract, he took a deposit,' she threw at him.

Any desire to laugh left him. He'd stood bail for the man's character and he'd let them both down.

'It's not the only one.' She leaned against the map table, as if standing up was suddenly too much effort, and he turned a chair, took her arm and eased her into it. 'I've spent half the morning going through his messages, his diary,' she said, looking up at him. 'He's taken deposits for at least a dozen other events and while no one else, apart from the bride, is threatening to sue, they do all want Rosie, or their money back.'

He could have said a dozen things but while most of them would have made him feel better, none of them would have been of any use to Lovage.

'Well, that explains why he didn't leave her with me,' he said grimly.

'Does it? What difference would it have made?' she asked wanly.

'I'd have told them to sue.'

She swallowed, even paler now. 'I can't do that.'

No. He'd got the message. Loud and clear. Basil was family and, while he might be a liability, he was *her* liability. Family was something to be cherished, protected.

It wasn't something he'd ever encountered on a personal level—he'd just been a problem. One that he'd had to solve in his own way.

'You didn't sign the contracts,' he pointed out.

'Maybe not and, to be honest, I'm not quite sure how I stand legally with everyone else but the film company contracted for Rosie. And she's now officially registered to me.'

'Would you like me to speak to them?'

She shook her head. 'The film producer isn't going to make my Christmas card list but where else is he going to get another Rosie at such short notice? It's just an hour of my time.'

'If you say so. What about the rest of the bookings?'

'I don't have the money to pay back the deposits,' she said. 'And the bride cried.'

'I'll bet she did,' he muttered.

'No… When her husband-to-be bought ice creams on their first date he gave her his chocolate flake. She knew right then and there that he was the one and only,' she explained.

'He probably doesn't like chocolate.'

'Sean!'

'Sorry.'

'Anyway, she wants to give him hers. It's to be a surprise. At their wedding,' she said.

'And I'll bet you cried when she told you that,' he said knowingly, folding himself up in front of her so that she didn't have to look up.

'No… Yes… Stupid.' She blinked, close to tears now, and he took her hands in his. They felt ridiculously small and they were shaking. And why wouldn't they? She'd been dumped on, threatened and been made responsible for fulfilling Basil's promises. Or paying back the deposits he'd taken.

And Sean had been an unwitting accessory.

Grasping her hands tightly to hold them steady, to reassure her that he wasn't going to abandon her to deal with this on her own, he said, 'Not stupid.' It wouldn't have done it for him, but he appeared to be in a minority of one when it came to the prospect of happy ever after. 'It's her big day and if she wants an ice cream van to make it perfect then she must have it. Just tell me what I can do.'

'Find Basil?' She raised long dark lashes. They were clumped together with the tears she hadn't been able to hold back and he lifted a thumb to wipe away one that had escaped, his hand lingering to cradle her cheek.

'I'll do my best,' he promised, 'but he could be anywhere.'

'Probably not in a duck pond, though,' she said, her mouth tucking up at the corners, a precursor to a smile.

'Probably not,' he agreed wryly. 'Did you have any luck with finding out what RSG means?'

She shook her head. 'I did wonder if it might be short for some casino where they were holding a high stakes game?'

'We seem to be thinking along the same lines,' he said. 'I'm beginning to have some sympathy with your grandfather cutting Basil out of his life.'

'He doesn't need your sympathy and neither do I,' she said. 'What I *do* need is a lesson in how to run the ice cream machine. It won't wait until Saturday.'

'That's why you're here?' Sean asked. Not to yell at him for getting her involved. Just to ask for his help?

'I'm sorry but your number isn't listed so I had to come and find you. And you're right, Rosie is cranky, at least until I got the hang of her.'

'I said she had her moods, but you're right, cranky probably is nearer. But I don't understand. I put my number on the message I left at the Blue Boar.'

Elle shrugged. 'I asked this morning, but no one could find it.'

'But I gave it to…' He shook his head.

'Who?' she demanded.

'Your boss.' He'd written a brief apology, along with his phone number, on one of the pile of paper napkins brought to mop up the spillage. 'He probably thought I was trying to pick you up.'

'Probably,' she agreed. 'I've worked there since I was eighteen. He still thinks of me as a kid needing to be protected.'

'Does he? I'd have said Sorrel was nearer the mark.'

'No,' she denied, much too quickly, a hot blush searing her cheeks.

'Well, you know best,' he said shortly, rising to his feet. 'Come on. Let's get out of here.'

As she got to her feet, he ushered her through the door. 'I'll be out of the office for an hour or two, Jess,' he said as he passed her door.

Elle stopped. 'I'm so sorry. I don't know what you must think of me,' she said to his secretary.

'Don't worry about it.' His secretary gave her a knowing look. 'I'm sure you had good cause.'

Elle turned to him. 'I barged into a meeting, didn't I? I didn't think. I was just so angry.'

'Jess is right. You had good cause,' he said, but she was frowning.

'I thought you were a mechanic?'

'I'm a bit of a jack of all trades,' he said evasively.

Jess's eyebrows rose slightly, but all she said was, 'Don't forget that you've got a meeting with Sir Henry at one.'

He checked his watch and turned to Elle. 'Did you come in Rosie?'

'It seemed like a good idea. Since I don't have an ice cream machine on my bike,' she replied, making a brave stab at sarcasm, which was a relief. Reproach he could cope with. Tears were something else. It also meant that he didn't have to go to Longbourne.

'It shouldn't be a problem,' he told Jess, 'but if he turns up before I get back—'

'I'll tell him that you were called away on a matter of urgency on the far side of the estate.'

'The truth, the whole truth and nothing but the truth,' he assured her, before pushing open the door to the courtyard where the staff vehicles—and Rosie—were parked. 'Actually, Basil has got one of those.'

Elle frowned. 'What?'

'A bike with an ice cream cabinet fixed to the front. The precursor of the ice cream van. He's been cleaning it up, getting it back into working order.' He risked a smile. 'He's still got some way to go.'

She leaned against Rosie's door. 'You know what, Sean?' she said, trying to match his smile but having a little trouble controlling her bottom lip. It took all his willpower not to take possession of it, still it with his tongue, make her forget all about her terrible morning. Forget everything. 'That's the first piece of good news I've had today.'

'Well, let's build on that,' he said briskly. She hadn't come here to pick up where they'd left off in the vanilla-scented interior of Basil's van. She wasn't looking for comfort either. Not the only kind he was capable of. She'd come for practical help.

Time, he could give her.

He'd have offered her the cash to pay back the deposits that Basil had taken if he'd thought for a minute that she'd take it. But he had seen enough of Lovage Amery to know that wasn't the way she did things. He wasn't going to assuage his guilt for getting her into this mess that easily.

She was going to honour Basil's commitments come hell or high water and if Basil Amery had walked into the yard at that moment Sean would have been hard pressed not to flatten him.

'Shall I drive?' he offered.

'Where are we going?'

'Somewhere we won't have an audience lining up for handouts the minute we start up the machine.'

Elle would normally have insisted she was capable of driving anything, anywhere, but she was still shaking. Not with rage, this time. This was far worse.

She couldn't shout at Basil, and kicking Rosie didn't help.

Sean had been the only person for her to yell at but, infuriatingly, he didn't have a listed number and she hadn't been able to pick up the phone and demand that he come to Gable End.

Instead, she'd struggled for ten minutes to start a very reluctant Rosie—who was undoubtedly bearing a grudge for that kick—and then driven the big van with unfamiliar gears through the narrow, winding lanes with impatient drivers hooting and gesturing furiously as she'd held them up. And there'd been no seat belt.

She didn't know where Sean lived on the estate, or how to find him. She'd had to stop at the main entrance and ask at the gate, where they'd directed her to the main office. More time wasted.

By the time she'd parked behind the wing that housed the main office, caught a glimpse of him through a window looking oh, so relaxed, she'd been about ready to explode. She'd waved off the woman who'd tried to stop her, storming into the office, but then he'd turned, looked up, a smile lighting up his eyes as if he was truly pleased to see her. Said her name with that whisper-soft drawl.

Not Elle, but *Lovage*.

He was the only person who'd ever called her that and for a moment, no more than a heartbeat, she hadn't been able to think.

She'd gathered herself again, almost immediately, but she hadn't been able to sustain her righteous anger. Not when he'd folded himself up before her, taken her hands so tightly in his, asked her what he could do to help. She'd just spilled it all out. She'd very nearly made a total fool of herself when she was telling him about the young bride. The girl had been so sweet, so in love. Of course Elle had cried...

And just now, when he'd stopped beside her, all she wanted to do was lean into his strength, for once let someone else take the burden.

But it wasn't Sean's problem. He'd simply delivered Rosie

as requested. She would rearrange her shifts as necessary. Get it done. Move on.

'Is it okay for you to just leave like this?' she asked.

'Don't worry, I won't get the sack if the boss hears I'm hanging out with the ice cream girl in office hours,' he assured her, unlocking the door, following her up into the cab. 'Knowing Henry, he'd just want to come and check you out for himself.'

Rosie started for Sean first time. No surprise there; Elle was pretty sure everything he touched started first time, including her.

They sped through the narrow, winding private lanes of the estate that visitors never saw before pulling into the parking area in front of a big old barn surrounded by a wild flower meadow. But not the workaday barn she'd imagined when he'd told her where Basil garaged Rosie.

One end had a pair of high double doors, sure enough, but two-thirds of it had been converted into a stunning home, with high windows looking out across the river. The kind of home that was often featured in upmarket homes and gardens magazines.

'Okay. First things first,' Sean said, wasting no time in heading for the business end of the van. 'The generator. It powers the lights, the freezer for the lollies and the ice cream machine.'

She watched while he switched it on, then took *Rosie's Diary* from her bag, carefully listing each stage of the procedure in the notes section at the back.

'I haven't got any lollies.'

'I imagine Basil picks up a supply from the cash and carry before each gig. You have to take them out when you've finished and keep them in a freezer, so you don't want to buy more than you need for immediate use.'

'Right.'

She started a second list. Lollies. She needed to count the stock she had. Would she have enough for all the bookings Basil had made?

Sean switched off the generator. 'Okay, now you try.'

She started it, following her notes to make sure she hadn't missed anything. It wasn't difficult, but he wasn't going to be around when she did this for real tomorrow.

'Got it. Now what?'

He showed her where to pour in the mixture, watched while she opened a carton and filled the tank.

'That seems simple enough.'

'It'll take fifteen minutes before you can deliver an ice cream. Just time for a sandwich and a cup of coffee,' he told her.

He didn't wait, but jumped down, unlocked the door to the barn and disappeared inside.

Elle found him in the kitchen. There were no units, just solid wooden furniture and shelves, rather like the old-fashioned kitchen at Gable End that had, thankfully, escaped a nineteen-fifties make-over and was now back in fashion. The only difference was that Sean's did not bear the evidence of generations of use. And his big American fridge wasn't decorated with fridge magnets holding photographs, messages, the shopping list.

Sean put the kettle on the Aga, took a loaf from a wooden bread bin. 'Cheese and pickle?'

Her stomach rumbled loudly at the prompt and without warning he grinned. 'I'll take that as a yes.'

It had been hours since the breakfast she'd thrown up and she suddenly felt hollow. Which no doubt accounted for all the wobbly leg stuff, the tendency to tears. She was just plain hungry.

'Can I help?' she offered.

'You'll find butter and cheese in the pantry,' he said, slicing the bread.

She fetched them, washed her hands, then buttered the bread while Sean sliced the cheese. He looked sideways at her. 'You've done that before.'

'I've made a few sandwiches in my time,' she admitted. 'Pulled a few pints.'

'Tossed a few rolls into diners' laps?'

'Jill of all trades, that's me,' she said, suddenly remembering the message he'd left for her. That Freddy hadn't given her and had denied ever seeing. 'Only particularly annoying customers get food thrown at them, though.'

'I'll bear that in mind.' Then, as he spooned coffee into a cafetière, 'What were you going to study at college? Before everything went pear-shaped?'

'Cooking.' She pulled a face. 'Somewhat ironic under the circumstances.'

'Tragic, I'd have said. So, what was the dream?'

'Dream?' she repeated, as if she'd never heard the word, never sat there, pretending, at the table she used as a desk...

'You must have had one. Your own restaurant? A Michelin star by the time you were twenty-five? Television chef?'

'Good grief, nothing that grand.'

He looked at her. 'No,' he said with a smile. 'That's not you at all.'

'Oh, thanks.'

'You would have dreamed of something warm, cosy—'

'If you must know,' she cut in before he could make things any worse, 'I had my heart set on an elegant little restaurant for ladies who lunch. Cloths on the table. Morning coffee. Simple lunches. Afternoon tea with freshly made sandwiches, scones, exquisite cakes. Good service.'

'Nostalgia squared.'

'Be careful what you wish for,' she said, layering on the cheese while Sean opened the pickle jar. 'Right now, I've got all the nostalgia I can handle.'

'Don't knock it. The estate shop makes a tidy profit from people who want jars of pickle, conserves that look as if their great-grandmother made them,' he said.

She glanced at the one he had opened, which bore a supermarket's own label. 'Not you, obviously.'

'I didn't have that kind of great-grandmother,' he said, slathering it onto the cheese. 'But plenty of people seem to go for it despite the high price tag.'

He fetched a couple of plates and mugs while she sliced the sandwiches neatly in half, then cleared up and wiped down on automatic.

'Do you want to take those outside?' he asked, pouring water on the coffee. 'I'll bring the mugs.'

'Don't trust me with anything that hot, hmm?'

'Am I that transparent?'

'Oh, yes,' she said, laughing. Then, unable to stop herself, 'At least on the surface.' She wished she'd kept quiet, but he was looking at her, waiting. 'You're quick to empathise, Sean, but you keep yourself hidden. I haven't a clue what you're thinking right now.'

For a second he was shocked into silence, then he said, 'Of course you have. I'm thinking that it's lunchtime and I'm hungry.'

'Point proved, I think,' she said, picking up plates and leaving him to follow with the coffee.

She walked through a room that rose high above her to the exposed beams of the barn. The floor was polished oak, the furniture was large, comfortable, old. The walls were pale to provide a simple backdrop for a dark Impressionist painting of a distant hill that was a prominent local landmark.

It had a clean, spare beauty that was in total contrast to the clutter of Gable End. A simplicity that gave away absolutely nothing about the man who lived there. No photographs. No treasures picked up on life's journey. No memories, no family. Except that wasn't right.

He'd told her that Basil had taken Rosie to his niece's birthday party. And a niece meant he had a brother or sister.

She opened high French windows that led out onto a paved terrace overlooking the river. The midday sun was sparkling on the water and, ignoring a couple of ancient Adirondack chairs that were placed side by side close enough for two people to reach out and hold hands, she followed a stepped path that curved away down to the river and a small dock.

CHAPTER EIGHT

Forget love. I'd rather fall in ice cream.
                                          —Rosie's Diary

SEAN took his time over the coffee. The lesson, he reflected, was never to ask a question to which you didn't want to hear the answer. He was practised at that. Good at keeping things light. People at a distance. Never digging beneath the surface to find out what made them tick. Taking care never to expose his own inner thoughts or feelings.

Elle challenged that in him. She told him stuff that he didn't want to know. Intimate, private stuff that seeped into his psyche, settled in the small dark spaces of his mind that had been left unoccupied. Stirring up the dust, disturbing the cobwebs.

He'd walked away from her yesterday, determined to stay away until Saturday morning. At the garden party, he rationalised, they'd be too busy to do more than pass out ice creams, take the money. And she'd be off to work as soon as he'd dropped her off and brought Rosie back to the barn.

Except Rosie wasn't coming back with him. And Elle was here right now.

He'd walked away, determined to put time and distance between them, but she'd come with him, lodged in his mind, stirring his body in ways that refused to be ignored. Driving him from his bed in the early hours to sit on the dock, his feet in the cold water of the river.

She'd been there when he woke.

His first thought had been of Elle, wondering what she was doing. How it would feel to turn and see her lying beside him. Hair tumbled over her pillow, lips soft, her lashes lying against her cheek. Every part of her totally relaxed in the total trust of complete surrender that letting go of consciousness in the presence of another person involved. It was why he never stayed overnight with any woman but always slept alone in his own bed. Refusing to give up that control to anyone.

It was why he'd fled the back of the van the minute they'd set the ice cream in action, leaving her to follow or not as she chose.

The memory of their last encounter in that small space was too vivid. The desire too intense.

He picked up the mugs. It would pass.

It always passed. His father, his half-brothers and -sisters demonstrated the fact on a regular basis. They were not a family with any emotional staying power.

And Elle was an emotional minefield. Best avoided but, if that was impossible, to be handled at long distance with the utmost caution.

He followed her through the living room, expecting to find her stretched out on one of the chairs on the terrace. But no. Typically, she'd ignored the obvious option and was down on the dock, leaning back, propped up on her hands, face to the sun, shoes off and legs dangling over the edge. Invading his space and filling his head with images that he wouldn't be able to get out of his mind. That would stay with him, haunt him, torment him.

She turned as the boards moved under his feet. 'This is lovely,' she said. 'Not what I expected.'

He didn't ask her what she'd expected.

'Do you fish?' she asked.

He shook his head. 'I leave that to the kingfishers. That's why the grass is left to grow over the bank so that there are shady places for the fish to hide.' Keep to the practical. He could handle that.

'I've never seen a kingfisher.'

'You have to be quiet. Still. Lie up in the grass further along the bank…' Instantly, his mind filled in the picture of the two of them lying in the long grass, touching close, waiting. And afterwards… After the vivid flash of blue, the kiss that would follow. And everything else.

No! The answer to her question was just… No. Keep it simple. Keep your distance.

'So why the dock?' she asked. 'The rowing boat?' And, gratefully, he seized on that.

'The dock was built to ship grain and wood down the river to Melchester. This is a tributary to the River May,' he added. 'As for the boat, I use it to keep an eye on what's happening with the wildlife, particularly the water voles and otters.'

'You've got otters here?' Her eyes lit up, sparking a dangerously hot response.

'They're making a comeback,' he said, sitting on the far side of the plates she'd set down beside her, using them as a safety barrier between them.

Better.

He bit into the sandwich they'd made together. Filling his mouth with food to keep himself from saying something stupid. Like inviting her to spend the afternoon with him. Offering to show her where the kingfishers were raising a family in a muddy hole in the riverbank.

Elle groaned as she took the hint and took a bite of her own sandwich, keeping nothing back. She said what was on her mind, her expression betrayed her every thought, drawing him in. Raising questions.

'Good?' he asked.

'Blissful. Wonderful cheese.'

'It's made in our dairy,' he said. 'We do good business in the farm shop.'

'We?'

'Developing income streams so that the house is self-sustaining is part of my job. We supply our home farm dairy products direct to the big London stores as well as local outlets,' he elaborated.

'So where do the vintage motors come in?'

'Nowhere. There were all sorts in barns and outbuildings all over the estate. Classic cars, farm machinery, old tractors. I was going to sell them off, but then realised that they could be a useful attraction. You've seen one Tudor beam, you've seen them all,' he said with a grin.

'I suppose.'

'Sorry if I misled you. I did find an old Morris that I got working one summer when I was about fourteen,' he offered. 'I taught myself to drive on the back roads of the estate.'

'Taught yourself?'

'No one knew I had the car. I hid it here. The barn was a wreck back then. Abandoned.'

A mallard with a flotilla of fluffy ducklings spotted them and came scurrying over.

'Oh, aren't they gorgeous!' Elle said, looking down as they gathered beneath his feet. 'They seem to know you.'

He shrugged, broke off a corner of his sandwich and dropped it to the mother duck, welcoming the distraction from old memories. Old hurts.

'I found a duckling that had been caught up in a plastic bag when I was a boy. It's so unnecessary, so annoyingly careless. I couldn't get anyone else bothered, so I began taking the boat out to clean up the rubbish that had been washed down from further upstream or blown in from the estate. I still do it myself when I have time.'

'No wonder Mrs Duck thinks you're a pal.'

'She only loves me for my bread and cheese. Try it.' She tossed in a few pieces of bread and found herself surrounded.

'Cupboard love,' she agreed, laughing.

'Is there any other kind?' he said.

'Don't you know?' she asked softly.

'Do you want to go for a walk along the bank?' he offered, needing to move, do something physical to get away from all this emotion spilling out. He didn't wait for an answer, but got to his feet, held out a hand. 'I can't promise an otter or a kingfisher, but if you keep very quiet...'

She grasped it, pushed her feet into her shoes, and he kept it fast in his as they walked along the bank, knee-deep in grass, late spring flowers. He pointed out a swan's nest on the far bank. Holes where water voles lived. A grebe and her family bobbing about beneath a weeping willow. Keeping it neutral.

'You clearly love it here. How long have you lived on the estate?' she queried.

That was the trouble with talking. It was like tossing a stone in the millpond. It hardly disturbed the surface and yet the tiny ripples it caused were unstoppable.

'I was born here,' he admitted.

'How wonderful to grow up with so much freedom.'

'I suppose.' No one had cared what he got up to as long as he didn't cause any damage. Or disturb the pheasants. It should have been an idyllic childhood. 'All of the fun, with none of the responsibility.'

So much for not saying any more.

'The late Baronet had a little midlife crisis fling with a secretary in his London office,' he explained. Better he told her himself than she learned it from someone else. 'He installed her in a weekend love-nest in one of the cottages on the edge of the estate.'

'Oh. I see.' She hadn't needed the connection spelling out. Nor had she responded with prurient interest or exclaimed over the fact that his father was a Baronet, even if he had been born on the wrong side of the blanket. 'Didn't his wife object?'

'She stayed in London and waited for him to get over it, which is probably why my mother played the pregnancy gambit. Bad decision.'

'Oh, come on, Sean. You don't know that's what she did.'

'It's a fair guess.'

'It was a love affair. Babies happen. Believe me, I know. And she chose to have you. Keep you.'

'Of course she did. I was her bargaining chip.'

'You are such a cynic.'

'And you are such a romantic. Sir Henry was never going to leave the daughter of an earl for a typist,' he said caustically.

She didn't say anything, just held his hand a little more tightly.

Her wordless empathy sparked a warmth that shimmered through him and it took him a moment to gather his thoughts, return to the expressionless recital of his history.

'He let my mother keep the cottage on a grace and favour basis, gave her a settlement to keep her sweet. It was in the days before an abandoned mistress's first action was to sell her story to the tabloids.'

'Does she still live here?'

'No. She was killed in a road accident when I was ten.'

'Oh, Sean… That's so tragic.' And this time she leaned against him so that it was the most natural thing in the world to let go of her hand and slip his arm around her. 'Tell me about her.'

'I…' He found himself floundering. No one ever asked him to talk about his mother. The cottage had been cleared when his mother died. Her clothes sent to a charity shop. Her personal belongings put in a box, stored away in the back of a cupboard somewhere. Her life brushed out of existence. 'She wasn't a happy woman.'

'I'm not surprised. It must have been horrible for her. Why didn't she go home to her family?'

'Not all families are like yours, Elle. They disowned her. Me. Sins of the flesh and all that,' he said gruffly.

'My family doesn't seem quite so great right now,' she said. 'What about your father?'

'Having got away with it once, he thought he had carte blanche but Her Ladyship did not prove so amenable the second time he strayed, rather more publicly, with a high profile fashion model, and he found himself free to remarry. He had three more children with wives number two and three before he broke his neck in a hunting accident.'

'That's a lot of family.' She sounded almost envious.

'Hardly family. I spent my early school years at the local primary being beaten up by the village kids for being "posh". Then, after my mother was killed, I was sent away to boarding school, where everyone took their lead from my half-brothers by treating me as if I was invisible,' he told her evenly.

'Kids can be so cruel. Where did you live?' she asked. 'When you weren't at school? Not with the family, I take it.'

'The adults only came for the shooting and Christmas. The kids were dumped here with their nannies for the holidays but I lived with the estate manager. His wife didn't like it but she wasn't about to say no to Sir Henry. The old man was okay. He kept me busy, encouraged my interest in wildlife, suggested I take a degree in estate management.'

'Definitely an outsider,' she said, but more to herself than to him. As if he'd answered some question that had been bothering her.

'Maybe,' he said, plucking a daisy, 'but this was my home in a way that it could never be theirs.'

'And now? What? You run the estate?'

'It never lets you down, never hurts you. It just is.'

'So you cherish it, keep it safe for a family who never gave you the love you deserved,' she said, as if pointing out the oddity in staying.

'They don't own it, Elle, any more than I do. It's entailed. Held in trust for the next generation. But, while they spend a few weeks a year here, I have it all the time. I control it, make the decisions, instigate the projects to keep it solvent for Henry, my half-brother and the present Baronet, to rubber-stamp.'

'Is that why he's coming today? To rubber-stamp one of your ideas? All the fun *and* all the responsibility.'

She was so wrong about not knowing what was beneath the surface, he thought. She saw right through him to the heart.

He grinned. 'All the fun and I'm paid for it too,' he replied as they reached the edge of the meadow and turned back.

'And with a fabulous old barn as your play house.'

He looked up at the barn. 'This doesn't go with the job. It's mine.'

'I thought the estate was entailed?'

'One of the advantages of living with the estate manager was access to the maps, the deeds. This stretch of land was bought much later, in the late eighteenth century. An add-on. Not part of the entail. I marked it out in my head as mine when I was fifteen years old.'

'They gave it to you?' she gasped.

'A gift to the dispossessed? I don't think so. I had some of the money the old man had given my mother, enough for a deposit, and I made an offer when Henry was being taken to the cleaners in the divorce courts. He could have sold the barn to a developer—a point he used to drive up the price—but he stuck with the devil he knew in the end.'

'Someone he trusted.'

'Yes. He knows where his best interests lie. But it's my footprint, my mark on the estate. More than any of his full brothers will get.'

'Are they resentful?'

'Not noticeably. They're all too busy running investment banks, or the country, and playing marital musical chairs to have time to spare for Haughton Manor.'

'That's a shame. A place like this needs people to bring it to life.'

'I suspect Henry would sell up to a sheikh or a pop star like a shot if he could, but he's stuck with it. It's my job to ensure that it doesn't cost them anything.'

'And the marital merry-go-round?' she probed gently.

'Not for me, Elle. I've seen enough marriage break-ups and confused, hurting kids to put me off the institution for good. I'm not about to join the party and add to the mayhem,' he warned her.

'Does your girlfriend know how you feel?'

'Girlfriend? Do you mean Charlotte?'

'If she's the dim one who believes that water will ruin linen, then yes.'

He laughed, enjoying the fact that she could be as catty as the next woman. 'Charlotte isn't my girlfriend. She's just a friend I sleep with occasionally. After her performance on Saturday, she's not even that.'

'A friend?' she asked. 'Or a sleeping partner?'

He looked at her. Her eyebrow was quirked up, but he suspected the question was more than casual interest. The thought warmed him.

'I don't do the second without the first,' he said, holding her gaze. 'And my friends don't usually take out their temper on someone who can't fight back.'

'Who?' She frowned, then, as the penny dropped, 'Do you mean me?'

'Who else?' And, without warning, it was suddenly too intense, too important. He pulled a face, managed a grin. 'Who knew that Freddy isn't ever going to sack you?'

'Oh, very funny,' she said, pulling away from his arm to gather up the plates and mugs. 'Come on. It's time to show me how to make the perfect ice cream cone.'

Sean, a cold space where a moment before there had been a warm woman, found himself wishing his half-brother and her ice cream to the devil. Wishing that he had the afternoon to show her the river.

There was no need to talk when you were drifting along with the current, letting it push you into the bank in some quiet place where you could forget about everything but the girl in your arms.

'All you have to do is press this button and the machine dispenses exactly the right amount of ice cream.' Sean was standing behind her, one hand over hers as she held a cone poised beneath the nozzle. With his other hand, he pressed the button and moved the cone beneath it as the ice cream descended.

It was hard enough to concentrate with his arms around her but then, as he leaned over her shoulder and took a mouthful of the result, his chin grazed her temple and she turned to look at him.

'Your turn,' he said.

'My turn?'

A smear of ice cream decorated his top lip. Without thinking, her reflex was to lick her own lip as she imagined how it would feel to lick it off. How it would taste. How *he* would taste...

For a moment she thought he was going to bend lower so that she could, but instead he dropped his free hand so that his arms were tight around her, took possession of the ice he'd made and replaced it with an empty cone.

'You try,' he urged, his hand still around hers, holding it steady.

Right. Ice cream.

He'd made it look deceptively easy but, with that image in her head, with him pressed against her back, she couldn't concentrate.

Her first attempt was more splodge than swirl, most of which would have fallen off if she hadn't caught it in the palm of her hand as it tilted sideways. He turned and reached for a bowl he'd had the foresight to bring with him and she dropped in the mess, took the damp cloth, ditto, and wiped her hands.

'You've done this before,' she said.

'I remember the mess I made of the first few, but practice makes perfect. The secret, as with most things, is not to rush it.'

'Absolutely.' She could pipe cream on a dessert and this couldn't be any harder than that. But when she'd piped cream in the Blue Boar kitchen she hadn't had Sean standing so close that she could feel his breath stirring her hair.

'Maybe if I try it myself,' she suggested, then instantly

regretted it as he stepped back, leaning against the counter, regarding her with eyes that seemed darker today.

She forced herself to turn away from the sight of his tongue curling slowly, sensuously around the ice cream, although, even with her back turned, the image remained, burned bright against her retinas. That was probably why it took her four more attempts before she produced a perfect cone.

'You're a fast learner,' he said as she finally indulged herself, letting the cool ice slide down her throat. Rosie had been standing in the shade, but it was still hot inside, even with the service window slid back. 'After your first effort I thought it would take most of the tank before you got it.'

'How many ices is that?'

'About twenty to a carton, I think.'

'Thanks for the vote of confidence,' she said wryly.

'I should warn you that when you take Rosie to kids' parties you'll need plenty of hand wipes because they'll all want to have a go.'

'You're quite the expert,' she commented.

'Hardly that, but my niece and all her friends did. Yet another reason why Basil left me to it. I was plastered in ice cream, chocolate sauce and just about everything else in that cupboard by the time they'd finished.'

'How old is she?'

'Daisy? Six.' He glanced at her. 'Why are you smiling?'

She shook her head. 'I was just imagining you swarmed with little girls all wanting you to show them how to make their own ices.'

'It was no laughing matter,' he said. But his mouth was calling him a liar. 'Believe me, I needed a very large Scotch afterwards to settle my nerves.'

'I don't think so.'

She was beginning to get the measure of Sean McElroy and she'd bet he'd been brilliant with them. Any boy who'd get mad enough about one dead duckling to take on the task of keeping the river safe for wildlife would surely grow up to be an ace uncle. A great dad, too, if only he dared to take the risk. Trust himself and come in from the cold.

Although definitely not with Charlotte. He was well rid of her.

She mentally slapped herself. The woman had been fighting for what was hers. It was what any woman would do. Not that it made any difference. The blonde was totally wrong for him. Or was that the point? If he was avoiding commitment, there was safety in being with someone so wrong.

'Why are you smiling?' he asked.

'Just thinking about you. And girls.'

'Don't say you haven't been warned,' he said, assuming she was talking about little ones. Probably just as well.

'You can come along and say I told you so, if you like.'

'You've got me for Saturday. Be content with that.'

'Saturday? But…'

'But?'

'Nothing.'

Everything.

The whole point of him coming along on Saturday was to show her how to operate the machinery and then take Rosie away afterwards. But he'd already shown her how to produce the perfect ice. And Rosie wasn't going anywhere until Elle had fulfilled Basil's promises.

He was still waiting and she pulled her shoulders together in what she hoped was a careless shrug.

'You don't have to come on Saturday now. Not unless you want to,' she added. Which was ridiculous. Why would a grown man want to spend Saturday afternoon dishing out ice cream?

He finished the cone, straightened. 'You really hate taking help, don't you?'

'Me? No…'

'You do everything. Run the house, cook, work all hours to keep everyone. You don't even want your sister to take a part-time job.'

'She's in her first year at college,' she protested.

'Most students have no choice, Elle. They have to get part-time work to support themselves. It looks good on their CV when they start looking for a job.'

'Not working as a waitress at the Blue Boar.' Although, according to Sorrel, she could do a lot better than that. 'It's important for her to concentrate on her studies. Make something of her life.'

'Because you missed out?' She didn't answer. 'Maybe you should be thinking about that, too. What are you going to do when they've left home?' He tucked a finger beneath her chin, tilting her face up so that she couldn't avoid his searching gaze. 'What about *your* dreams, Elle?'

She swallowed. Right now, with him standing this close, there was only one dream in her head and it had nothing to do with cupcakes.

'I'll think about that when they're both through college.'

He shrugged, let go, stood back. 'Fine. Be a martyr if that's what you want.' She'd scarcely had time to draw breath and object before he added, 'They won't thank you for it and you're not going to be much use to them if you break down trying to do everything.'

'I'm not being a martyr,' she declared. She was just doing what had to be done. 'I'm all they've got.'

'Geli is as old as you were when you took on responsibility for the family.'

'Are you saying that I've done my bit and now I should off-load it onto her?' she demanded.

'No.' Then, 'Ignore me. I don't know what I'm talking about. Just accept that, like it or lump it, you've got me on Saturday. It'll be a long afternoon,' he said before she could object—and she really should object. 'Anything could go wrong.'

'Thanks. That really fills me with confidence.'

'You'll be fine. You just need a little practice on some real customers. Come on. You can give away some ice cream. Make a few people happy.'

'But…'

'The alternative is throwing it away so that I can show you how to dismantle the machinery for cleaning,' he warned.

'Haven't you got to get back to your meeting?' she asked, close to caving in.

'I'll meet, you serve and then we'll come back here and finish the lesson.'

He didn't give her time to argue, or consider what lesson he had in mind, but climbed behind the wheel and headed back in the direction of the Manor. As they got nearer, he said, 'Time to drum up some custom.'

'Does that mean I get to play the jingle?'

'You'll have to learn how, first.'

'Okay,' she said, looking over the dashboard. 'What do I push?'

'Push?'

'I assumed there'd be a button or something. To start the disk?'

'Disk? Please! This is a vintage vehicle, madam. Built before the age of seat belts and the Internet,' he said.

'Oh, right. The Dark Ages. So, what do you do?'

'This,' he said, taking hold of a handle beside him in the driver's door. 'You wind it up here, then switch it on and off here.' He demonstrated and a ripple of 'Greensleeves' filled the air. 'Your turn.'

Elle regarded the far door. To reach the chime she'd have to lean right across Sean. Get dangerously close to those firm thighs and what was undoubtedly a six-pack beneath the soft linen shirt he was wearing.

'I can't reach,' she said cravenly.

He leaned back in his seat. 'How's that?'

'It would be far too dangerous while we're moving,' she said primly. Miss Sensible.

His response was to slow down, pull over. 'We're not moving now.'

'It's still—'

She broke off as he put his arm around her waist and slid her across the worn, shiny seat so that she was nearer the door. Nearer to him.

'How's that?' he asked, looking down at her. 'Or would you like to be a little closer?'

'Any closer and I'd be in your lap!' she said, laughing, then let out a shriek as he slid his hand beneath her knees.

'No! I can manage,' she exclaimed. Possibly. If she didn't think about the fact that her cheek was on his shoulder, her breast mashed against his ribs, her shaky leg tight up against his rock-hard thigh.

She swallowed. Tried not to think about the warmth of his body against hers. The way his hand fitted into her waist and just how good it felt there. About the fact that she could hear the slow, steady beat of his heart. It had to be his, because hers was racketing away like a runaway train.

'Are you sure you can reach?'

'Mmm…' She could reach but, for some reason, she'd forgotten how to speak. 'Do you want to give it a go, then?'

'What?'

'Oh, the jingle!' She would have blushed, but her entire body was already flushed from head to toe. 'Absolutely!'

At least she'd regained control of her tongue. Whether she could keep her hand steady as she eased it through the small space between the steering wheel and an even more dangerous intimacy remained to be seen.

It felt like that party game where you threaded a loop over a wire that would buzz if you touched it. Would a buzzer go off if her wrist brushed against the denim stretched tight across his hips?

'Got it,' she said with a little gasp as she reached safety, winding up the mechanism the way he'd shown her. Not moving, but remaining tucked up against him as the tinny notes of 'Greensleeves' once more floated out across the parkland.

It was over too soon.

'Again?' he asked and she laughed, looked up and her eager

yes died on her lips as she realised that his mouth was mere inches from her own.

This close, in this light, she could see a deep crease at the corner of his mouth that must once have been a dimple, tiny flecks of green in the blue, giving his eyes the colour of the sea on a perfect day. The scar above his left brow.

The potent scent of his warm skin overlaid with vanilla was making her light-headed and she reached out, traced the jagged line of it with the tip of her finger.

'How did you get this?'

'I can't remember. Maybe it was when I fell out of a tree.'

'Ouch.'

'Or when I crashed my bike.'

She caught her lip.

'Or in one of those playground fights. It still hurts a bit,' he added. 'If you felt like you wanted to kiss it better.'

She didn't hesitate. She lifted her head an inch and her lips found his. Or maybe he'd come to meet her halfway. She didn't know, didn't care, only that as he pulled back to look down at her she wanted more. More kisses. More of him.

Was that how it had been for her mother? That rush of desire flooding through her veins? Making her breasts tingle, her lips burn for a man's touch? Making her feel powerful, in control...

'I remember now,' he said, his voice so low that it seemed to vibrate through her, setting off a chain reaction that spread out to every part of her body. 'It was definitely the tree. I also broke my collarbone.'

'Here?' He caught his breath as she slid her hand beneath the open neck of his shirt, feeling the shape of the bone, pushing it back so that she could lay her lips against the warm skin.

'I cracked a couple of ribs too and there was a terrible bruise...'

CHAPTER NINE

A world without strawberry ice cream? That's a world without summer.

—Rosie's Diary

A SHARP rap on the window jerked Elle back to reality. She banged her elbow on the steering wheel as she disentangled herself, then she was back in her seat, pink, dishevelled, flustered, while Sean slid back the window.

'Henry?' Sean said, calmly acknowledging the man who'd rapped on the window.

'Sorry to interrupt when you're so obviously busy, Sean, but I haven't got a lot of time.'

'Hang on, we'll be right with you.'

Sean, apparently not the least embarrassed or flustered, drove into the staff car park, angling the van across three spaces so that the serving window was facing the centre of the courtyard.

A silver Range Rover pulled into a space next to them and Henry, who looked so much like Sean that he couldn't be anything other than his brother, climbed out.

'So, what's going on here?' he asked as Sean slid back the serving hatch, giving her a chance to catch her breath, fan the heat from her cheeks.

'Charity, Henry. The way it works is that Elle will give you an ice, while I relieve you of a donation for the Pink Ribbon Club.'

'Oh, right!' he said, laughing. 'Walked right into that one, didn't I?' He offered her his hand. 'Henry Haughton.'

'Elle…' She cleared her throat. 'Elle Amery. How d'you do?'

'Amery?' He glanced at Sean.

'Basil's great-niece,' he explained. 'She's standing in for him.'

'I'm not complaining.'

'You may not say that when you see the mess I make of your ice cream,' Elle said, taking a starched white coat from a laundry bag, several sizes too big, she'd found in one of the cupboards. Perching a cap on her head.

'What can we get you?' Sean said. 'A vanilla cornet with all the extras?'

'I think you're the one getting the extras,' Henry said, grinning, as he took a wallet from his back pocket. 'I'll pass on the ice, thank you, Elle. But put this in the kitty for your good cause.'

He handed her a note and she stared at it. Fifty pounds?

'Thank you, Sir Henry. That's incredibly generous.'

'Henry will do. Any girlfriend of Sean's—'

'Is a girlfriend of Sean's,' Sean cut in sharply.

Henry shrugged unrepentantly. 'No harm in putting in a bid, is there? I rather like that milkmaid look.'

'You'll be okay?' Sean asked her as his brother headed into the office.

'Fine,' she assured him.

'Any problems just—wind up the jingle.'

Before she could answer, he'd jumped down, heading for the office.

Girlfriend…

'No…' He'd got that wrong. Sean didn't have girlfriends; he just slept with girls who were his friends.

And the problem with that was…?

As if her hot, vivid thoughts had reached out and touched him, he turned in the doorway, looked back. One corner of his mouth tilted up in a smile as if he knew exactly what she was thinking, as if he was thinking much the same thing. Her heart jolted as if it had been hit by one of those cardiac paddles that were the mainstay of hospital dramas. And not just her heart.

Desperate, Sorrel had said and maybe she was right. But Freddy was never going to generate anything like that reaction inside her body.

Not if he—or she—lived to be a hundred.

'Pretty girl,' Henry said as they walked towards the office. 'Deliciously…buxom.'

'And all mine,' Sean said without thinking.

His brother raised an eyebrow. 'That's unusually possessive of you.'

'Just warning you off before you get any ideas. How are your domestic arrangements these days?' he asked pointedly.

Henry smiled. 'Not a lot of fun. Hattie is pregnant.'

Pregnant? It took him a moment before he gathered himself sufficiently to respond. 'Well, congratulations. I had no idea you were contemplating adding to your brood.'

'Hattie's idea. Second wives,' he added, as if that said it all. But he was smiling nevertheless. His potency confirmed.

'She's well?'

'Morning sickness morning, noon and night. I thought I'd seen the last of that. But she's through the first three months, the scan is good and I'm allowed to share the news.'

'She must be so happy.'

'Ecstatic. When she's not being sick. But it's going to mean a few changes. I'm going to be easing back on work in the City, spending more time here.'

'Oh? Problems?'

'No.' He shrugged. 'Yes… Banking isn't what it was but there'll be a nice golden handshake and I'm going to sell the London house, buy a flat instead.'

'Well, you seem to have everything worked out. And it will be good to have a family living in the house. I've noticed how the public respond to that lived-in warmth when I've been to look at other historic houses,' Sean said.

'Hattie suggested we might do weddings.'

'Definitely problems.'

'That would be intrusive,' he pointed out. 'If you're going to be living here. The Manor isn't that big.'

'In the Orangery, she thought. I said she'd have to talk to you. And Olivia had some scheme she's mad keen on, too,' Henry said.

'We did exchange a few words on the subject.'

'I heard.'

'She's split up with that idiot she's married to, Sean. She didn't want me to tell you. You're so judgemental, but if you could give her a little slack?'

Judgemental? Was that him? Walking around with a holier than thou attitude? Sean wondered in dismay.

'Just find her something to keep her mind off things. She'll soon lose interest,' Henry said.

'Occupational therapy.'

'Exactly. I can leave that to you, then?'

Sean glanced out of the window to where people were gathering around the ice cream van. He could see Elle laughing as she handed the estate surveyor an ice, completely at ease, but then she spent her life dealing with the public.

She looked across, as if aware that he was watching her, and he knew exactly what she'd say to him if she was standing beside him.

Half-sisters are family, too. To be cherished, kept close.

It was what she'd done. Taking responsibility for them all, giving up her own dreams, her own chance of a family, because there weren't many men who'd take on that kind of baggage. Troublesome teens, an ageing grandmother losing her grip on reality.

He, on the other hand, had spent his entire life keeping his family at arm's length, watching as their marriages fell apart and feeling smugly superior.

But while they'd got it wrong more times than not, they hadn't been afraid to take the risk. Or pick themselves up and try again.

Was he, after all, the loser?

'I don't suppose there's any chance that you'll settle down soon?' Henry asked, leaving the question unanswered. 'You seemed to be pretty close to the girl in the ice cream van just now,' he said, looking out into the courtyard. 'That is a smile that would be a pleasure to come home to. Very welcoming. On the other hand, there's nothing wrong with a romp in the hay.' He shrugged. 'After all, you do live in a barn. Where is Amery, by the way? Not done a bunk, has he?'

'His rent is paid for the quarter. He's gone away for a while, leaving Elle to hold the fort. I've been showing her how everything works.'

'And doing a very thorough job, I noticed.'

'Watch your mouth, Henry.'

His brother smiled, clearly satisfied with the response he'd provoked. And Sean's prickly reaction was proof that his brother was right on target. Henry's broad grin suggested that he knew it too, but he didn't push his luck, just said, 'Remind her that Basil always put in an appearance at the Steam Fair at the end of the month.'

'I don't think…' he began, then let it go. It was probably one of the bookings in Basil's diary. 'Tell me,' he asked instead, 'do the initials RSG mean anything to you?'

Henry considered for a moment. 'Royal something or other? Society, maybe.'

'Unlikely, I'd have thought.'

He shrugged. 'Try the Internet.'

'Well? How did you do?'

Elle's smile was as wide as the Cheshire cat's.

'Fourteen more or less perfectly turned out ices, all with

chocolate flakes or sprinkles. Fourteen happy customers. And, along with your brother's contribution, a total of a hundred and twenty pounds for the Pink Ribbon Club.'

Sean whistled. 'Did I say you were a fast learner?'

'The Haughton Manor staff are incredibly generous. Obviously they were prepared to pay for the ices, but when I told them that the ices were free and all I wanted was a small donation for a very worthwhile cause...'

Her smile, impossibly, widened and she lifted her shoulders, practically to her ears, so totally delighted that he wanted to pick her up and hug her. She was just so thrilled. Nothing held back. His brother was right. She had a smile you'd want to come home to.

'Don't forget to take out your costs,' he warned, fighting off the impulse to go for it, make it his. He'd been telling himself that it was Elle he was protecting by keeping his distance, but it wasn't anything that noble.

He was the one who'd be left hurting if it didn't work out. Abandoned. Even as he yearned for her touch. The natural, eager, open-hearted warmth that had got her mother into so much trouble.

He needed to keep it practical. Feet on the ground.

'Diesel, supplies,' he added.

'Oh, but I couldn't—'

'You must. You'll have to replace the ice cream mixture, buy fuel,' he reminded her as he turned away to settle into the driving seat. Start her up. Keep his mind, his hands busy. 'You're giving your time, Elle. No one expects you to subsidise the charity. Or Basil. You can't afford it.'

'I suppose,' she said, slightly deflated, as she settled beside him.

'Just keep clear records, receipts, so that you can prove what you spent to the taxman.'

'No problem. I'm used to accounting for every penny,' she said, even more dispiritedly. Then, making an effort, 'I liked your brother.'

'Women always do, but then he always reacts generously to a sexy smile. It's why his first wife divorced him.' Then, instantly regretting his cynical response to what had been a genuine reaction to Henry's generosity, 'You caught him on a good day. Wife number two is expecting a baby.'

She frowned. 'You don't approve?'

'Not my business.' He was clearly going to have to work harder at being a warm human being if he was going to pass Elle's empathy antenna. 'He said it was Hattie's idea, but he seemed pleased with himself.'

It wasn't the reaction his own birth had evoked and a shadow crossed Elle's face, too. No doubt she was thinking about the unknown father she had sought out year after year at the Longbourne Fair.

His own father had been a very distant figure, but at least he had taken responsibility for him.

Elle, however, shook off whatever dark thought she was har-bouring and laughed. 'I know what your problem is. You've just realised you're going to have one more little niece or nephew to plaster you with ice cream.'

'A nephew, I hope. They're more likely to grab an ice and run. Not like little girls, who want to decorate them.' Decorate him. He glanced at her. 'On the downside, Olivia, one of my numerous half-siblings, has split up from her husband.'

'I'm sorry.'

'It was her second marriage. My family seems to feel single-handedly obliged to keep the statistics dynamic.'

'With you as ballast.'

He glanced at her. 'That's pretty much what Henry said.' Then, afraid that he'd said too much, 'He also reminded me that Basil is expected to bring Rosie to the Steam Fair we hold in the park over the long holiday weekend at the end of May. Is it in the diary?'

'The weekend was blocked out, but Basil hadn't written anything in.'

'I suppose he thought I'd tell you.'

She turned to look at him, then, 'Why? He's taken a lot for granted, Sean,' Elle said. 'We're family, but why would you bother?'

Sean had asked himself the same thing. Why had Basil got him involved with all of this? They were acquaintances with a shared interest in old vehicles. Basil allowed him to buy him a pint now and then at the Haughton Arms. But this went way beyond that.

'Maybe,' he said, struggling for an answer, 'maybe he thought it was time I did.'

'Bother?'

Bother. Get involved. Get a life. Not end up like Basil, old and living on his own.

'You did explain the situation?' she asked. 'To your brother.'

'You'll make a mint of money,' he pointed out, avoiding a direct answer. Because he hadn't explained. He wanted her in the park for three whole days. Wanted her close enough so that he could look up and see her in the place he called home. Look up and smile when she saw him.

'*Basil* will make a mint of money,' she retaliated. 'If the sun shines. All I'd get out of it is three days when I couldn't go to work. When I wouldn't be paid.'

'Read the letter again, Elle. Basil transferred ownership of the van and all that went with it to you. He made it clear enough that whatever you earn is yours. And the Steam Fair is for enthusiasts who come from all over the country. A drop of rain won't put them off.'

'But…'

'What kind of deposit did Basil take for his bookings?'

'I don't know about the film company, the man wasn't exactly chatty, but the bride told me she'd given him a non-refundable twenty-five per cent deposit. Twenty-five per cent of what, I have no idea,' she added.

'Enough to cover the cost of buying supplies,' he suggested thoughtfully. 'Presumably he did that for every booking. He has left you well stocked. Ready to go without any outlay.'

'You're saying that he's used the money to start me—well, Gran—up in business?'

'He didn't normally do more than one or two events a month. He wouldn't have needed that much.'

She frowned. 'But…'

'It was a hobby for him, not a business and he turned away a lot more bookings that he accepted. With all the bookings he's lined up for the next couple of months… Well, it suggests he might have been thinking along those lines.'

'I thought he'd taken the money and run,' she said dazedly.

'Apparently not.'

'But if that's the case, why didn't he give us the paperwork on his clients?' she demanded. 'Explain what he was doing more clearly? Why did he just disappear?'

'I've no idea, but I suspect he knows a lot more about you than you realise. Maybe he thinks it's time you got out of the Blue Boar and chased your dream?'

'I promise you,' she said frankly, 'I never dreamed I'd be driving an ice cream van for a living.'

'But that's not what you'll be doing,' he pointed out. 'You've got bookings from a film company, for a wedding, and didn't you say there was some kind of business do as well as the more usual kids parties?'

'A business do and a retirement party,' she admitted.

'Then you haven't got an ice cream round, Elle. What you have is an events business.'

She opened her mouth to protest, closed it again. Then she looked at him. 'Where is he, Sean? What is RSG? I'm getting really worried about him.'

Sean took her hand for a moment, an instinctive gesture of comfort. But, even as he did that, he began to suspect that what Basil was doing was playing games. The old man wanted to be back in the comfort of his family home, the centre of attention, but he'd made some promise he couldn't break.

* * *

Upper Haughton was the kind of picturesque village that decorated biscuit tin lids. No intrusive modern street lighting or
yellow lines painted on the road and, since there was only one
way into the village from the main road, there was no through
traffic to cause problems.

All it needed to become the fictitious village in a nineteen-
sixties drama series was for the modern cars and signs to be
removed before the cameras could roll. Since it had already
been used in a picturesquely rural detective drama, and the
parish council had been handsomely rewarded for the incon-
venience, the villagers knew the ropes and were, on the whole,
happy to co-operate.

Elle had become intimately acquainted with every part of
it throughout a very long morning.

'An hour should do it', Kevin Sutherland had said. Ha!

She'd turned up in good time but it had been two hours
before anyone took any notice of her. She'd then spent an age
trying to teach the idiot actor how to produce an ice cream that
anyone would want to eat, trying not to think about Sean, his
arm around her as he'd taught her to do the same thing.

Finally, she'd driven around the green dressed in a white
coat and peaked cap so that from a distance it would look as
if it was the actor driving the van while the director filmed
'establishing' shots. Playing the jingle and trying really, really
hard, not to think about how she'd kissed Sean. Bold as brass.
A proper little hussy...

It would have been fun but for the fact that she was supposed
to be at work at twelve and it was already half past. She couldn't
even phone and let Freddy know she'd be late. The production
assistant had locked her cellphone away before she was allowed
on the set. The last thing they needed, apparently, was for one
to start ringing in the middle of a 'take'.

And now, just when she could escape, she'd been grabbed
by a reporter from the *Country Chronicle*, the monthly county
magazine. She assumed it was because everyone else was too
busy, but apparently not.

'We're doing a major feature on the filming and we're particularly interested in any local businesses that are involved,' she said. 'It'll be good publicity for the county. Bring in visitors.'

She doubted whether a picture of her and Rosie would do much for the local economy but, irretrievably late for work, she answered questions and posed for pictures with Rosie, ice cream in hand.

Then, before she could escape, the local television news team took her place. She smiled and went through the same routine with them. This time with the ice cream dripping over her fingers.

She binned the ice cream, licked her fingers and took the sheet of paper that the production assistant handed her, along with her phone.

'Thanks, Elle. Sorry it took so long, but you were great.'

'No problem.' She looked at the paper. 'What's this?'

'The shooting schedule for the rest of series one. I've marked the days we'll need Rosie.'

'Series *one*?' Elle looked at the list, saw half a dozen days highlighted. 'I thought this was a one-off?'

'Good grief, no. The ice cream guy is having an affair with the wife of the landlord of the pub. Lots of tension.' She smiled. 'It's edgier than the usual nostalgia stuff for this period—mostly sex and horses combined with crooked local politics and murder. The networks are salivating.'

Elle wasn't quite sure what to say, other than *help*.

'Rosie is part of the cast,' the woman continued, as if this was something she should be glad about. 'And, heaven forbid, even if the show does fold after series one, it'll still be great publicity for you.'

Publicity!

'Here's your payment pro forma. I've attached my card. Send your invoice direct to me and I'll make sure it goes through quickly.'

On the point of telling the woman that the last thing she needed was publicity, Elle saw the amount on the pro forma.

Three hundred pounds, less the seventy-five that Basil had already been paid as a deposit. For one day. And not even a whole day.

She swallowed. Hard. Managed a strangulated, 'Thanks.' Cleared her throat. Three hundred pounds. An events business. 'I'll get right on to it.'

CHAPTER TEN

*Put 'eat ice cream' at the top of your list of things to do
today and you'll get at least one thing done.*
                                                —Rosie's Diary

SEAN couldn't concentrate. All he could think about was Elle.
How she'd looked as, relaxed, her bare feet dangling over the
edge of his dock, she'd lifted her face to the sun. Her concentration as she'd tried to fill her first ice cream cone. The pink flush
to her cheeks as she'd leaned across him to reach the chime,
looked up, kissed him. When he'd kissed her.

He should be grateful to his brother for coming along when
he had or the heat they'd been generating would have melted
the ice cream.

Fortunately, there was nothing like a meeting with Henry
to remind Sean why he never got involved with anyone. And
Elle didn't have time, even if he'd wanted to. She'd needed to
get back to Longbourne to be there when her sisters got in from
school. Another good reason not to get carried away.

She was not his kind of girl. Not free to flirt, free to stay or
go as she chose. And yet this morning, when he should have
been focusing on building plans for an extension to the dairy,
all he could think about was whether she was managing Rosie
on her own and how the filming was going. The softness of her
lips. Her fingertips walking along his collarbone…

It was as if she'd taken up residence in his head, distracting

him, filling his thoughts in ways that no other woman had
ever managed.

He picked up the phone to call Olivia, suggest she come
down to Haughton Manor so that they could discuss her ideas
for the stable block. Anything to take his mind off Elle. And
he found himself dialling Elle's number instead.

His call went straight to voicemail.

Instead of hanging up, he listened to her voice, seeing
her face, her eyes as she invited him to leave a message.
Remembering the way she'd licked her upper lip, seeking out
a crumb of chocolate, and how he'd hardened in immediate
response.

'Elle...' He hadn't intended to leave a message, but her name
escaped him before he could stop it. 'Just checking that everything went okay this morning. I'm doing my best to chase down
Basil.' And still he didn't hang up. 'See you Saturday.'

He tossed the phone on the desk.

Pathetic. A fifteen-year-old boy could have done better.

'What's for tea?' Geli asked as she walked through the back
door.

Elle looked up. 'Good grief, is that the time!' She usually
heard the Maybridge bus pulling into the village, had the kettle
on before her sisters had crossed the road, but the afternoon
had flown by.

She hadn't taken Sean's suggestion that she had an embryo
events business seriously but when she'd got home yesterday
afternoon she'd unloaded most of the boxes from Rosie's interior, ready for the film set this morning. Tucked away behind
them, out of sight, she'd found a box file containing Basil's
paperwork.

There wasn't much. Simple accounts, his invoices, receipts
from suppliers, an account card for the local cash and carry. She
hadn't had time to look at it then. She'd barely had time to put
together supper before she'd left for work, but as soon as she'd
got away from the film set she'd called Freddy and, claiming

a family crisis—Basil *was* family and he'd disappeared; that surely had to count as a crisis—apologised for missing her lunchtime shift.

He'd been so concerned, insisting that she take the evening off as well, that she knew she should be feeling a lot guiltier than she did. But today she had other things on her mind.

Sean, for one...

He'd asked for her number in case he heard from Basil, but she hadn't expected him to call her just to ask how things had gone this morning.

She'd longed to call back, tell him about it, that it wasn't a one-off contract, that it was more important than ever that Basil was found so that she could be sure what he'd meant when he'd transferred Rosie to her. His casual 'See you Saturday' suggested he didn't expect—or want—that and she pushed away the memory of standing beside him, working together as they made a sandwich for lunch.

Refused to dwell on the small joy of sitting beside him on the dock as he'd told her about his family. Shared his pain. Tried to forget how he'd wrapped his arms around her to demonstrate how to produce the perfect ice cream...

It was the possibility of starting her own business that was the big one.

Her mind might keep wandering off, wondering what Sean was doing right now, counting off the days until Saturday, but she'd yanked it back into line. Done what she'd always been good at and concentrated on reality.

'What's all this?' Sorrel asked, picking up the sheet of paper on which she'd been brainstorming names for her embryo company.

If she was going to have a business, it wasn't going to be a hobby.

'Scoop? What's that?'

'Not Scoop, but *Scoop!* In italics, with an exclamation mark.'

'I'm starving,' Geli said, dumping her bag. 'What's for tea.'

'Open a tin of beans,' Elle said distractedly, waiting for Sorrel's reaction to the name.

'*Scoop!*' Her sister lifted an elegant brow. 'This is for Rosie, I take it?'

'You're not going to start an ice cream round?' Geli demanded, horrified.

'No, an events business. I've got some bookings.'

Geli rolled her eyes but Sorrel put her laptop on the table, pulled out a chair and sat down. 'You know there's a big market for this kind of thing. A lecturer at college hired an ice cream van for her little girl's birthday party last month.' She thought about it. 'It could have been Rosie.'

'Where's the tin opener?' Geli asked.

'For heaven's sake, it's in the same place it's been for the last fifteen years.'

She got a 'huff' and a noisy opening of drawers in response.

Maybe Sean was right. She did do too much for them. She hadn't expected anyone to open a tin for her at that age. On the contrary. She'd been the one coming in from school and getting tea for everyone else.

'What kind of bookings?' Sorrel asked.

'A surprisingly wide range.' She ran through them, determinedly ignoring the bad-tempered clatter from Geli. 'And the icing on the cake is that Rosie is now a member of the cast on the television drama series they're filming at Upper Haughton.'

'What?' Geli's scorn dissolved in an instant. Beneath the bored exterior, the pale face and black charity shop clothes, there apparently lurked an ordinary teenager who was just as impressed with fame as the next girl.

'That's what I was doing all morning. The *Country Chronicle* took photographs.'

'Excellent,' Sorrel said. 'We can use that on flyers and the website.'

'Website?' Whoa...

'I think we should have a blog, too. *Rosie's Diary*?' She

looked up. 'Time to put your IT skills to good use, Gel. You *can* spare us some of your precious time to design something and get us online?'

'Will I get paid?' she demanded, quickly recovering her disdain.

'Of course you'll get paid,' Sorrel replied before Elle could stop her. 'You'll be tax deductible. Make a note of the time you spend. We'll work out an appropriate hourly rate later. We'll need letterheads and invoices, too. Something simple, neat…'

'Okay, but I can't work on an empty stomach,' Geli said pointedly.

'You'll have to be registered for VAT,' Sorrel said, ignoring her. 'I can probably do that online.' She lifted her laptop onto the table and began to makes notes. 'This is so great. Exactly what I need for a project. *Setting Up a Small Business*.' Then the cool mask slipped and she grinned. 'You do realise that we are going to need a broadband connection?'

'What?' Elle looked at the pair of them. 'Let me get this right. You'll help me, but only as and when it suits *you*? For money, or because it will make a neat college project and it means you'll get broadband? Well, thanks. Thanks a bunch.' She stood up. 'You know what? This is *my* business and if I'm going to have to pay someone "an appropriate hourly rate"…' she did that really irritating quote mark thing with her fingers because she wanted everyone else to be as hacked off as she was '…I'll get a professional. Someone who knows how to open a can of beans.'

The room fell silent and, without warning, she could hear Sean saying, 'You really hate taking help, don't you?' She'd denied it, but it was true. She just didn't trust anyone else. It wasn't only about money, it was everything. Shopping, cooking, cleaning. If she didn't do it herself, it wouldn't be right…

For years she'd done it all. Been not only sister, granddaughter, but mother to all three of them. They took and took and took and it was her own fault for letting them. For not making them do their own washing, get their own food. Because she wanted to make it up to them. Losing their mother, the stuff that they took for granted. Be...perfect.

But Lavender had been *her* mother, too. Adorable, funny, warm, but not perfect. Far from perfect. And she wouldn't have done all this. Wrapped them in cotton wool. Spoon-fed them.

'It's...um...done,' Geli said tentatively. 'Shall I open another tin? Make beans on toast for everyone?'

'That would be great,' Sorrel said. 'And put the kettle on. I think we could all do with a cup of tea.'

Elle, torn between the need to curl up in a corner and bawl her eyes out or burst out laughing, sucked her cheeks in.

'You think you can buy me off with baked beans and tea?' she asked, trying to be tough.

'It's a start,' Sorrel said. 'Now, tell us about *Scoop!*, which is a totally brilliant name, by the way. We'll listen and then you can tell us how we can help.'

'Actually, you were just about there,' she admitted. I realised I'd need a website, but the blog is a great idea, especially with the filming.'

'What are you going to wear?' Sorrel asked.

'Well, Rosie is early nineteen-sixties vintage and I thought... Do you remember the trunk full of our great-grandma's clothes we used to dress up in? They are the right era. Late fifties, early sixties.'

'Oh. My. Goodness. You're right. They would be just perfect. They'll need a good wash. Shall I see to that?' Sorrel offered.

'Maybe you should start with something a little less challenging laundrywise,' Ellie suggested. 'But I'd welcome a hand with the formalities.'

'I'll make a list.' Then, 'Are you going to give in your notice at the Blue Boar?'

'Not immediately. Let's see how it goes. Is something burning?' Elle asked.

Before either of them could answer, the door opened and

her grandmother appeared from the morning room where she'd been dozing away the afternoon in front of an old movie.

'Elle,' she said, looking surprised. 'You're here.'

'I've been here all afternoon, Gran.'

'But…' she looked back into the morning room '…you're in there. On the television. Talking to a reporter on the local news.'

They all rushed into the morning room, but the news had already moved on to another item.

'You *were* on the television,' she insisted. Elle was about to explain when the telephone rang.

Sorrel picked it up. 'Oh, hello, Mrs Gilbert. Did she?… Did you?… For your granddaughter's birthday? I'm afraid Elle isn't here at the moment,' she said, cool as a cucumber, holding Elle off. 'I'll ask her to check the diary and call you back first thing in the morning. No problem.' She turned to Elle. 'That was Mrs Gilbert. The woman who owns the garden centre? Mrs Fisher was talking about Rosie in the post office—'

'I'll bet she was,' Geli interjected dryly.

'—and then she saw you on the television. I would have taken the booking but I had no idea when Rosie's free, or what to charge.'

'How old is her granddaughter?' Elle asked.

'Good point. And I should have asked how many children they've invited. That's going to affect the cost. We're going to need a see-at-a-glance wall chart for bookings. And a price list,' Sorrel said.

'I can work that out now I have Basil's paperwork.'

'Who's Basil?' Geli asked.

'Basil…' Her grandmother grabbed for the back of an armchair but, as Elle and Sorrel exchanged a desperate look, she seemed to gather herself, straighten her back. 'Basil,' she said, 'is Grandpa's brother. Your great-uncle.' Only then did she let Elle ease her back into the armchair.

'But…Grandpa didn't have any brothers,' Geli said.

'Just one. They were chalk and cheese. Bernard was an

engineer, captain of the local rugby team. Big, strong, sports mad. The kind of man every girl wanted to be seen with. Basil was a couple of years younger, artistic, a bit of a clown, but all the girls adored him, too. He was so easy to be with.' She shook her head. 'It was all an act, of course. The clowning. I found him one day by the village pond trying to work up the nerve to end it all. Silly boy.'

'Why?' Sorrel asked. 'Why would he do that?'

Elle threw her a warning look, but her grandmother was oblivious. In a world of her own as she remembered the past.

'He'd been going out with a girl from Lower Haughton, but only so that he could be near her twin brother. He knew he was gay and it terrified him.'

'But that's awful,' Sorrel gasped.

'The law had changed by then, but attitudes hadn't. He couldn't bear the shame of his parents knowing. Bernard… He was his hero.'

'So what happened? Where has he been all these years?' Geli asked.

'I let out his secret. The girl he'd been going out with was my best friend. She adored him and I didn't want her to get hurt,' their grandmother revealed.

'*You* told her?'

'We were at a party and she was all over him. I couldn't bear it. I told Basil he had to tell her or I would. Bernard overheard us. He thought I was playing fast and loose with the two of them and he'd followed us to find out what was going on. I sometimes think he only married me to keep the secret in the family.'

'Secret?'

'Basil went home and faced his father. The old man told him that he had to leave. Disappear. Never come back, never contact the family ever again.'

'Just like that?' Elle asked.

'He gave him money, a lot of money, but it wasn't right. If his mother had still been alive, I'm sure things would have been different. I don't think Bernard ever forgave himself for what happened. Or me.'

'Oh, Gran,' Elle said sadly.

She looked up. 'I was just trying to help.'

'Of course you were.'

It explained so much, Elle thought, as she hugged her. And made it even more imperative that she find Basil. Bring him home.

'The beans!' Geli yelled.

Later, when they'd got rid of the smell of burning beans and the ruined saucepan, Elle retired to the privacy of her own room to call Sean.

'Elle? Is there a problem?'

'No,' she said. Nothing could be wrong when she was lying on her bed with his voice rippling through her, soft and warm as melted chocolate. 'Not wrong, exactly. Just different.'

'How different?'

'Are you sitting comfortably? It's a long story.'

He listened while she filled him in on the family secrets.

'How do you feel about that?' he asked when she'd finished.

'Sad for them all. But it explains a lot about why Grandpa was the way he was.'

'Life is endlessly complicated.'

'I suppose.' She settled lower against the pillows. 'But the odd thing is that since she's told us Gran seems…I don't know… more…here.'

'She's been living with that guilt for a long time. Telling you must have felt like a weight being lifted from her. You did say that the doctor told you she was blocking out what she couldn't deal with.'

He'd remembered?

'Mmm… We're all feeling a bit giddy at the moment, I think, but it's more urgent than ever that we find Basil and bring him home.'

'Of course. Do you want me to search the cottage? I only glanced through the place before, just to make sure he hadn't taken an overdose and was lying... Well, you know.'

'I know,' she said.

'You could come over tomorrow and we could do it together, if you like? We could reprise the cheese sandwiches. Feed the ducks again. Maybe take the boat out.'

'That is so tempting.'

'Haven't you heard? You should always give in to temptation,' he teased.

'I really wish I could.' Then, realising that she might have been a little too eager, added quickly, 'You've done so much already.'

'And you've already missed an entire day's work.' He sounded a touch off. 'Freddy will be missing you.'

'Rosie isn't going to replace my job, Sean. Not yet, anyway. I have bills to pay.'

'I know. Leave it to me. I'll see what I can find.' Changing the subject, he said, 'So, tell me about today. How does it feel to be a television star?'

'Rosie made the evening news, I'll have you know,' she said. 'And she's going to be featured in the *Country Chronicle*.'

'Hot stuff.'

'You'd think so, but it isn't like that.' And at his prompting she told him all about the filming. The endless waiting around. Had him laughing at her description of the good-looking but thick actor who couldn't make a ice cream cone to save his life. Doing things over and over again.

'It doesn't sound as much fun as you'd think.'

'Mostly it was just mind-numbingly boring,' she admitted, 'although it did get a lot more exciting when I discovered how much they were paying me.'

'That will do it every time. So are you beginning to take me seriously?' he asked.

'Absolutely,' she said without hesitation. He was so easy to talk to, share things with that, before she knew it, she'd told him about her plans for Rosie. The name she'd thought up.

'Scoop?'

'With an exclamation mark. What do you think?'

'I like it. Short, snappy, memorable. Make sure you have some flyers with you on Saturday and we'll spread the word.'

'The girls are working on them now.' Then, reluctantly, 'I suppose I'd better go and see how far they've got.'

'Let me know if you need anything printed,' he offered.

'That's really kind of you, Sean, but if we're going to be a serious business we need to get ourselves properly organised.' Then, when the silence went on a moment too long, 'This is not me being unable to accept help. I am making an effort to let go a little. Trust my sisters. Other people.'

'Me?' he asked. 'Do you trust me?'

The question was so unexpected that for a moment she floundered.

'You're wise to hesitate.'

'Am I?' she asked. 'What exactly are we talking about here?'

'We've already covered the question of money,' he reminded her.

Elle opened her mouth, closed it and, heart beating just a little faster as she ran her tongue over dry lips, said, 'What else is there?'

He didn't answer. Her call?

She swallowed. Her heart was pounding in her ears now. 'I'm sure that a man so determined to avoid commitment must practise safe sex.'

'Sex is never safe. Not if the emotions are engaged.'

Was he warning her that while men could be uncommitted, emotionally disengaged—that *he* would be uncommitted— women were always going to be hurt?

'Life is not safe, Sean. My mother died young, but she filled every moment of her life with…life. By the time she was my age, she'd had lovers, children.' Heartbreak, maybe, risk, but joy, too.

'You're not like her, Elle.'

'How do you know that?'

'You need a forever man who'll make you the centre of his life.'

'Her father, my grandfather, was a forever man,' she told him. 'And I wouldn't want the life my grandmother lived with him either. Meantime,' she said, moving on quickly because he'd made it more than clear that he couldn't handle 'forever' and assumed she couldn't handle anything else, 'if I'm going to run *'Scoop!'* as a serious business I have to do this properly. Not rely on favours from friends.'

'I thought you were learning to take help? Yours wouldn't be the first local business who'd used our copier in an emergency,' he argued.

'If there's an emergency, I promise I'll call you. And I would still like you to look after Rosie since you know her so well. But not in return for ice cream.'

'And if I insist on being paid that way?' he asked, his voice teasing, evoking the memory of his tongue curling around creamy ice. 'Rosie and all the works as a birthday treat.'

'For your many nieces and nephews?'

'I was thinking of something a little more…personal.'

'Oh…' As she lay there, her skin was so sensitive that every inch of clothing was a torment, her lips burned for the cooling touch of his ice-chilled mouth. Her breasts felt heavy and the ache between her thighs, the hot poke of desire, made her reckless. He might not be interested in commitment, but then she wasn't free to give it and, without stopping to think, she said, 'Well, if those are your terms, I'd have to do my best to fulfil them,' she said, so softly that she might have been talking to herself.

'You see how easy it is?' Sean said, and even though she couldn't see him she knew he was smiling.

'But I get to choose how it's served,' she went on, as if he hadn't spoken. 'Exactly where to pipe the ice cream…'

'Elle…' He wasn't laughing now.

'Where to drizzle the chocolate fudge sauce.' He uttered one word that assured her that she had his full attention. 'A special one made with coffee liqueur. I love coffee liqueur…'

'Excuse me, Miss Amery, but are we having phone sex?' he asked, his own voice pure Irish cream.

'Elle!' Geli yelled from the bottom of the stairs. 'I need you to look at what I've done.'

She sighed. 'With my family, it's the only kind we're ever likely to have.'

'You're forgetting my birthday.'

Geli was thundering up the stairs. 'Elle! Where are you?'

'No.' She wasn't about to forget this telephone conversation. Ever. 'When is that? I need to make a note to keep the evening free.'

'I'll leave that up to you,' he said. 'Whenever you have a spare afternoon or evening just…call me.'

'Elle!' Geli burst in, then stopped. 'Oh. Were you asleep?'

'Maybe,' she said, rolling over, pushing the phone out of sight beneath her pillow as she swung her legs to the floor. 'Just give me a minute. I'll be right down.'

She splashed her face with cold water. It wasn't enough. Her body felt aroused, as if Sean had been there in the room with her, lying beside her, touching her, undressing her. It was going to take a cold shower to bring her back to earth.

CHAPTER ELEVEN

Six or sixty, it still hurts when your ice cream falls from its cone.

—Rosie's Diary

SEAN tore off his T-shirt, shucked off his jeans and plunged naked into the river.

The cold hit him like a blow, but the fire Elle had stoked up in him refused to die down and he swam upstream until it felt as if he were warming the water, rather than the other way around.

His brother was right. Lovage Amery had a smile to come home to. A voice that warmed him through, touching something buried so deep inside him that he hadn't known it was there. Even now was afraid to examine too closely for fear that it was an illusion.

She was a woman who had taken everything that life could throw at her and still took on emotional complications without reservations. No caveats or conditions. No ifs or buts…

No fear.

She had that from her mother, he suspected. It was the wholehearted grasp on life that had somehow eluded him.

They were complete opposites in that. He'd taken a step back, determined not to break her heart, but he'd completely misunderstood her.

Elle might cling obsessively to physical security, but she

gave love as if it came from a bottomless well. Would risk her heart without a second thought. While he was prepared to risk anything but. Hoarding his feelings like a miser, protecting them from danger, keeping them locked away until they were stunted, miserable things without value.

She was ready to come to his bed if he wanted her, and there was no doubt that he wanted her.

But forever?

How could you know, be sure? Or was that what she was telling him? That you couldn't ever be certain, but it was worth the risk anyway.

He stopped fighting the river and let it carry him home, but as he reached the dock he discovered he was not alone.

'Wild night-time swimming isn't going to do your cold any good,' Charlotte said, stepping in front of him so that he could enjoy a close-up of her stunning ankles. 'Just as well I came bearing honey and lemon.'

'I never saw you in the Florence Nightingale role,' he said, pulling himself out of the water, forcing her to step back or be showered. Using his T-shirt to dry himself.

'You have me,' she admitted. 'I was lying about the honey. But then we both know that your sudden cold on Saturday night was of the diplomatic variety.'

'The chill was real enough,' he assured her and she sighed.

'I know. I came to apologise for being such a catty witch, Sean.'

'In that case you're in the wrong place. It was Elle who could have lost her job.'

'Elle...' For a moment she hesitated as if there had been something in the way he said the name that betrayed him. Then, as if dismissing the thought, she arched her brow and said, 'Oh, please. Her boss had his hands all over her.' She'd noticed it, too? 'Very possessive. If she's in trouble it's your fault for flirting with her.'

'Pots and kettles, sweetheart,' he said, reaching for his jeans, pulling them on. 'You always make a point of flirting with good-looking waiters.'

'Maybe I do, but I never look at them the way you were looking at her.'

He didn't argue. Charlotte flirted in the same way she breathed. Without thinking about it. He only flirted when his interest was engaged. And Lovage Amery had grabbed his total interest from the moment she'd opened her front door to him.

When he didn't respond to her needling she let it go. 'Oliver Franklin was at the party on Saturday. I let him take me home.'

'Did he give satisfaction?' he asked idly.

'I didn't...'

'No, of course not. He's on the list of men you might eventually marry. You need to keep him eager.'

'He asked me to have dinner with him one day this week,' she said, offering him one last chance to change his mind. 'I said I'd call him.'

'Do that. You've kept the poor sap at arm's length for long enough.' Her face betrayed her. 'You'd never settle for me, Charlotte. I don't have an estate of my own, a title, money. I'm just someone you're filling in time with while you scope out the market.'

'And the waitress will, I suppose.' She sounded forlorn, but she didn't deny it. 'It's time to grow up. Take the next step.'

She sighed. 'Is that what's happened to you?'

He didn't know what had happened to him, only that the type of relationship he'd enjoyed with Charlotte wasn't enough for him any more. As he leaned close enough to kiss her cheek, he said, 'Be sure to send me an invitation to the wedding.'

She gave a little shiver. 'I don't think so.' Then, 'It's hard, isn't it?'

'Growing up?'

'Falling in love. But you're right. You're fabulous in bed, but you're not husband material.'

She didn't wait for an answer but turned and walked away, her heels beating out a sharp staccato on the dock.

She was wrong, he thought, as he stretched out on the dock, staring up at the stars, the sound of her little roadster racing through the estate roads growing fainter and fainter until the night was reclaimed by small insects, a nightjar, the occasional splash of a small river mammal. So wrong.

Falling in love wasn't hard. Compared to not falling in love it was a piece of cake. That required concentration. Lose it for a moment and love slipped unnoticed under your defences as sweetly, as effortlessly as an ice cream sliding down a parched throat on a summer's day. No drama or noise. Just a smile, a touch, a kiss was all it took to bring down even the most powerful fortifications, so that without warning you were falling, with nothing to grasp hold of.

He'd still been hot and horny when he'd emerged from the river and a repentant Charlotte, eager to make up, should have been a gift. A week ago he wouldn't have thought twice. A week ago his life had been simple.

Today there was only one woman he wanted in his bed. Not just for an hour or two, but to wake up with. He wanted to open his eyes and see Elle's hair spread over the pillow. Her lashes lying against her cheeks. See her open her eyes and smile.

But forever?

It was clear that, like his brother, he'd reached some kind of turning point. He just wasn't sure where this new turn was taking him.

A tap on the dining room door on Saturday sent Elle's heart swooping up into her mouth, her hand flying, scattering the leaflets she was piling up across the table.

'Sorry. I didn't mean to startle you. Your grandmother said I'd find you in here,' Sean said.

'You didn't startle me. I saw you pull in.' Saw him jump down from the Land Rover he was driving today.

She was in the old dining room, empty since the bailiffs

had carried away the Regency dining room suite, the china, the silverware that had once graced it. Now it was the *Scoop!* Office-cum-store room with cartons of cones, pallets of ice cream mix piled up at one end.

Leaflets, boxes of stationery that had been quickly run off on the printer at the Small Business Unit set up in the college were on an old bookshelf they'd moved down from one of the bedrooms.

A large planner was pinned to the wall so that they could see all their bookings at a glance but the pièce de résistance was the rail of clothes that they'd brought down from the attic. Glamorous Madmen dresses from the early sixties.

For the Pink Ribbon Club, she'd picked out a dark pink dress with a sweetheart neckline, nipped in waist and a full skirt that was exactly Rosie's era. She'd pinned up her hair in a classic chignon. Painted her lips and nails bright pink to match her dress.

Sean had played his part. He was wearing a black T-shirt with the word '*Scoop!*' written in pink sparkle across his chest. The fact that it exactly matched the fonts Geli had chosen for the flyers and their letterheads could not be coincidence.

'You've been cross-referencing our designs,' she said, weirdly shy after the intimacy of their phone call. The kiss they'd shared. She was never tongue-tied, but it was as if she didn't know what to say. As if he didn't know what to say.

They hadn't spoken since then. He'd only sent a text telling her that he hadn't found anything useful in Basil's cottage. She'd sent one back saying thanks for looking. It was as if they'd almost stepped over some precipice and were wobbling on a dangerous edge and it could still go either way. One wrong word and it would all be over.

'You look absolutely amazing, Elle.'

'A bit different to the usual get-up,' she agreed, self-conscious in such unaccustomed finery, so much make-up. Maybe that was it. All starched up, she didn't feel like herself.

'You've been busy.'

'Yes. Panicking mostly.'

That raised a smile from him. Better. She began to relax.

'I saw the website. And the blog. *Rosie's Diary*? I thought Rosie sounded very like you,' Sean said.

'Did she?'

She wanted to ask him what she sounded like. Whether he liked it. Wanted him to put his hand on her cinched-in waist, pull her closer, kiss her neck. Maybe if they lost themselves in desire everything would be all right, but the mind-reading thing didn't seem to be working today.

'I'm not sure that's a compliment,' she said finally.

'Aren't you?' The smile lines deepened imperceptibly. 'Jess enjoyed it. And my sister, Olivia, loved the stuff about the filming.'

'Your sister? The one whose marriage broke up?'

'She's got an idea for craft workshops in the old stable block and needs something to keep her occupied.'

'And you're letting her play with your estate?' she asked incredulously.

'She'll soon get bored, but I thought, what would Elle do in this situation?'

'Now that is a compliment.'

He shrugged. 'What harm can she do?'

She let her hand linger briefly on his shoulder. 'None at all, Sean.'

He took her hand, kissed her fingers, kept hold of them. 'You did a great job of selling the PRC Garden Party. On the blog. It was both funny and touching…'

She swallowed. It had been hard writing that.

'I've ordered some Rosie badges,' she said, eager to change the subject before a tear that had been threatening all day ruined the sixties eyeliner that Sorrel had applied so carefully. 'To give away at children's parties.'

'Turning them into walking advertisements for your business? Nice one,' he approved.

'And of course we have the retro clothes.'

'They're fabulous,' he said, flicking one-handedly through the rail, stopping at a glamorous full-skirted halter neck black lace dress. 'Where did they come from?'

'The attic. We used to dress up in them when we were kids. Mum used to do our hair, make us up. I thought I'd wear that one for the evening events,' she added. 'With very high heels and bright red lipstick. What do you think?'

'I think that the businessmen will believe they've died and gone to heaven,' he said. 'And the old guy at the retirement party will probably have a heart attack.' He turned to look at her. 'I'm in danger of having one just thinking about it.' Then, as if he'd said more than he meant to, 'Hadn't we better go?'

She gave a little yelp as she checked her watch. 'Can you bring those leaflets?'

She didn't wait for a reply, but practically fled the room.

Sean gave himself a moment, gave her a moment, but as he gathered up a pile of leaflets advertising *Scoop!*, he saw the smear of pink on his thumb where it had rested close to her mouth and, unable to help himself, he rubbed it against his lower lip, tasting it. Tasting her.

Forget about some old guy having a heart attack when he saw her in the black lace. He'd come close when he'd seen her in the pink dress and there was a lot less of her on show in that one.

There had been a moment, no more than a heartbeat, when Elle had turned and her entire body had appeared to lift in welcome. Or maybe it had been his own instinctive response to the sight of her. An urge to reach out and touch her. Just a hand to her arm. The kind of small, intimate gesture exchanged by lovers.

They weren't even close. They'd shared just one kiss. So why did he feel more like her lover than he ever had with any woman he'd known?

What was this intimacy that had nothing to do with sex, lust? This belief that he knew her? That somehow her thoughts, her feelings mattered more than his own? The powerful draw that brought him back to her even when she'd told him to go.

All week, wasting precious time hoping to find some small clue, he'd cursed Basil up hill and down dale. But Basil was the one excuse he had to keep coming back to her. Even when the risk of it scared him witless. Even when he needed no excuse.

It was Elle who'd led the way on the phone, boldly teasing him, making promises.

She was such a curious mixture. Capable in ways that the Charlotte Pickerings of this world could never imagine. A woman who'd learned very early in life to deal with loss, officialdom at its worst, hardship, she would hold the world at bay to protect her family.

'Sean!'

He smiled at the imperious summons in her voice.

Not a curious mixture, a glorious one.   She deserved to be wooed, courted, made to feel valued. He might not be able to give her the kind of commitment she deserved, but he could at least give her that.

'Sean!'

'Right with you,' he said, following her into the kitchen where she was standing holding up the retro pink kettle he'd bought her.

'What,' she demanded, 'is this?'

'A kettle?' he offered.

For a moment their eyes met and he dared her to turn it down.

'Thank you.' She turned quickly away. 'Sorrel is coming along with us to learn the ropes.'

Her sister glanced at her. Clearly it was the first she'd heard of it but she was quick on the uptake. 'Can't wait.'

'Just Sorrel?' Sean asked, not entirely sorry to have a little chaperone to keep things from boiling over. They needed time. They needed space. 'What about you, Angelica? Aren't you desperate to learn the trick of producing the perfect ice cream?'

'I'm too busy tweaking the website and blog,' she said, flicking her mouse and leaning sideways so that he could see. 'I'm putting some of those cute things Basil wrote about ice cream in Rosie's speech bubbles at the head of each page.'

'Neat idea. And that's a great cartoon of Rosie. Who did that?'

'Me,' Geli said, doing her best to look cool, but failing miserably. 'I'm going to take arts and design at college.'

Elle, helpless to stop herself, drank in his profile, the straight nose, firm chin, long fingers as he leaned forward, raking back the dark hair sliding over his forehead with long, slender fingers. Trying not to think about what they could do to her.

Instead, he took the mouse, clicking through the pages until he paused on one and looked up, catching her before she could look away.

'Everyone has a price—mine is ice cream...?' His right brow kicked up. 'Basil wrote that?'

'He must have been thinking of you,' she said and was finally rewarded with one of his killer smiles. The kind that sent heat surging through her veins, leaving her shaky, helpless.

But the mention of price reminded Sean that he had something for Elle and, taking out his wallet, he produced a cheque. 'I sold your car.'

'Did you advertise it on the Internet?'

'No. I emailed a description to some enthusiasts I know. It's not a lot, but this way you don't have to pay commission.'

Elle took the cheque, looked at it, then up at him, eyes narrowed in suspicion. 'Not a lot?'

'She's an old classic and while she had a few internal problems, her bodywork was in amazingly good condition. I'd have made more if I'd had time to do some work on her, but I thought you might need it now,' he told her.

'Thank you again.' Then, turning to Geli, she said, 'Take care of this. It's your trip to France paid for and enough for a driving school car to take Sorrel through her test next week.'

And, having handed the cheque to Geli, she took Sean's hand, wordlessly, in her own for the briefest moment.

'Okay. Time to go.'

At the garden party, Sean watched Elle add a frilly white apron to her outfit.

'One of your delicious ices, please, Miss Amery. Something very pink if I'm going to be a walking advertisement for your wares.' He stretched out his arms to display the sparkly logo emblazoned on his chest. 'No one I pass will be able to resist the temptation.'

He saw her swallow down whatever she was going to say. 'Would you prefer a shell or a cone?' she asked.

'Give the man a cone,' Sorrel said, then, when Elle glared at her, she rolled her eyes. 'It would do it for me.'

Elle decorated the ice lavishly with pink mini marshmallows and sprinkles, then wrapped the cone in a pink paper napkin. 'Is that pink enough for you?' she asked as she handed it to him.

'I'd have liked to have seen a few crushed beetles,' he teased as he put down his money.

He could see that she was dying to tell him that he didn't have to pay, but she pressed her lips together to stop the words and, by then, a queue was forming.

He licked a groove up the side of the ice, sucked the top into his mouth. 'If you have any problems, get the announcer to...' he met her eye '...call me.'

For the first hour Elle didn't have time to think, which was just as well. If she'd had time to think, Sean's provocative 'call me' would have had her melting faster than her ices.

Not that he'd rushed back.

From her high viewpoint, she'd caught glimpses of him from time to time, working his way through the crowd, always talking to someone or other. He seemed to know an awful lot of people. Most of them women. One of them was the blonde with the linen dress from that evening in the Blue Boar.

She tried not to look, but couldn't help herself. Not that they talked for long. The blonde turned and headed for the car park. And finally Sean headed for her.

'Everything okay?' he asked. 'No problems?'

'None,' she admitted.

'You can cope if I shoot off? Bit of a panic back at the estate.'

The mind-reading thing worked two ways, she discovered. The fact that he was lying was coming off him in waves.

'Another baby duck in distress?' she asked sweetly, calling herself all kinds of a fool for all the angsty thoughts she'd had just an hour or so earlier. She didn't wait for his lying answer, but waved him away. 'Don't get your feet wet.'

He frowned and she thought he was going to say more, but he let it go, raised a hand to Sorrel, turned and walked away.

'What is it with you two?' Sorrel asked.

'I don't know what you mean,' Elle denied.

'You look at one another as if you want to tear each other's clothes off and yet you're keeping each other at arm's length.'

If only.

'Sean doesn't do commitment, Sorrel.'

'So?'

Pretty much what she'd been thinking until he'd looked her in the face and lied.

'Just leave it,' Elle said, turning to serve someone.

The Royal St George Golf Club was on the far side of the country on the south-east coast. Charlotte had got his round robin email asking if anyone knew what RSG might stand for. Apparently Oliver played golf and had been to the Open the last time it had been played there.

And Sean had seen some golf trophies in Basil's cottage.

He'd tried phoning, but they'd refused to give any information about members or guests, which meant that he had to go there.

He hadn't told Elle where he was going because he hadn't wanted to get her hopes up. Just as well. He'd been clutching at straws and now he was stuck in a motel with a toothbrush and cheap razor from a slot machine instead of sending out for a takeaway and spending the evening with Elle and her family, sitting out beneath the lilac tree, with the blackbird serenading them.

And, with luck, getting a kiss goodnight for his trouble.

He checked his watch. Picked up his mobile phone and called her. Listened to her phone ringing until it was picked up by voicemail. Listened to her asking him to leave a message, but then cut the connection. There was no message. He had nothing to tell her. He just wanted to talk to her, hear about her day. Hear her laugh.

Tomorrow. He'd call her in the morning, tell her where he was, what he'd done. What an idiot he was.

Elle had looked at her phone when it rang, seen the caller ID and left it to be picked up by voicemail.

It had been a good day and a bad day.

Until Sean had left Longbourne Court to follow the blonde home it had been a pretty good day.

They had made a lot of money for the PRC. Exactly how much she'd work out in the morning. More than enough not to feel guilty about having to deduct costs.

All the leaflets had gone, thanks to Sean, although how many were now trampled into the grass for the Longbourne gardeners to pick up remained to be seen.

But it had gone downhill from there. Sean hadn't returned and when they'd packed up just before six, Rosie decided to sulk. By the time Elle had managed to get the trick of coaxing her into life, her day had hit rock-bottom. And when they did get home, only she knew how to dismantle the ice cream maker, how to clean and disinfect it. Only she had a precious hygiene

156

certificate—now stuck up beside Basil's inside Rosie—thanks to her stint working in the Blue Boar kitchens.

Then she had gone to work. Late again.

How could he?

She didn't expect a forever commitment from a man she'd met only a week ago, who had given her fair warning that the word wasn't in his vocabulary but, no matter how short it was to be, it had to be total commitment while it lasted.

It seemed he couldn't even manage that.

She ignored the phone for as long as she could before, unable to help herself, she picked it up. Called up her messages.

Nothing.

Sean hadn't bothered to leave one. Not even a simple goodnight and, despite the warm night she shivered, rolled off the bed and closed the window to shut out the heavy scent of the lilac.

CHAPTER TWELVE

Don't drown your sorrows. Suffocate them with ice cream.

—Rosie's Diary

ELLE got up early when she heard Geli making a move. Made her breakfast before she went to do her dog-walking stuff, then shut herself away in her office to rationalise the accounts for the PRC charity.

She checked stock, making a note of what they needed to reorder, and kept herself busy making a cake as a treat for everyone. They deserved it.

Doing her best not to think about the previous Sunday when she'd slept in, got up when everyone else had gone out. When Sean McElroy had walked into her kitchen and turned her world upside down.

Difficult with that pink kettle gleaming across the kitchen at her. With her pink dress hanging in the scullery waiting to be washed in the morning. With Sean leaning against the frame of the open door.

Geli had left it open when she'd rushed off to walk her waifs and strays and after a night shut up in her bedroom Elle had been glad of the fresh air. She really was going to have to start locking it.

'Hi,' he said. 'Something smells good.'

'I made a cake.'

'You are a domestic goddess. Any chance of a cup of tea to go with it?' he asked.

'It's too hot to eat, but help yourself to tea,' she said, waving in the direction of the kettle. 'You know where everything is.' Proud of the fact that she'd managed to control the wobble in her voice. 'You look as if you've had a hard night.'

He rubbed a hand over his unshaven chin. 'You could say that,' he said, pushing himself away from the door. He checked that there was water in the kettle and switched it on. Pulled out a chair and collapsed onto it.

Now he was closer, she could see that he looked exhausted. 'Duck give you a hard time, did she?'

'Duck?' He managed a grin. 'Not a duck. It was a wild goose. I didn't have a problem at the estate, Elle, but then you already knew that, didn't you?'

'I knew you were lying to me, if that's what you're asking.'

'Yes, well... The truth is that I drove to Kent yesterday afternoon.'

'Kent?' That was on the other side of the country and if he'd driven there and back since yesterday afternoon it was hardly surprising that he looked exhausted. 'Why?'

'I send out an email to everyone I know asking if they knew what RSG might be. Someone suggested Royal St George. It's a golf club.'

He'd driven all that way just to find Basil?

'Let me guess. The someone would have been Charlotte?' He looked up. 'I saw you talking to her. Just before you left.'

'Someone she knows suggested it. She gave me a lift home so that I could pick up my car.' He smiled wryly. 'She didn't know it was for you or I doubt she would have bothered.'

'Probably not,' she said dryly. 'Does Basil play golf?'

'There were some trophies in his cottage.'

'Recent?'

'Nothing since nineteen seventy-five.'

'And for that you drove what, four hundred miles, on the off chance that he might still be playing?' she exclaimed.

'He might have been there. Then I'd have been a hero instead of an idiot.'

'Stay with the idiot,' she advised. 'RSG could mean anything.'

'I know. I spent most of the night surfing the 'net and discovering just how many anythings it might have been.'

'Such as?'

'The Red Star Garage?'

'Basil comes to you for spanner work,' she reminded him.

'Ridge Side Gardens. Rodney, Simmons and Garth. Roundabout Servicing Guide…'

'It's a Rumpelstiltskin puzzle, Sean.'

He looked confused.

'Like the name in the fairy tale,' she said. 'Off the wall. Unguessable. Reorder Sparkly Gravel. Ring Supermarket for Gravy. Retrieve Second Gargoyle.'

'Reverse, Stop, Go?' he suggested, grinning as he caught on.

'Far too sensible. Ribbons—Silver and Gold…' She stopped. 'Actually, that makes some kind of sense. I've got those on my own shopping list. For the wedding. And the hen night. Why didn't you tell me?' she asked. 'Where you were going. I would have come with you.'

'Would you? What about Freddy? You'd have missed work.' He shook his head. 'I didn't want to get your hopes up.'

'My hopes can handle the occasional disappointment.' She wasn't sure she could take another evening, night, believing that he'd abandoned her for another woman. 'But thank you.' She leaned forward and kissed his forehead. 'Do you want some breakfast?'

'Actually, all I want right at this moment is to hold you, kiss you, then lie down and go to sleep for ten hours. But breakfast would be good to be going on with.'

'Breakfast can wait.'

She stood up, held out her hand and, as he took it and stood up, she turned and walked through the house, up the staircase, into her bedroom. She closed the door, then, her heart pounding like the entire timpani section of the London Philharmonic Orchestra, she said, 'Hold me.'

'Elle…'

She lifted her arms, put them around his neck.

'What are you doing?' he asked, putting his hands around her waist.

'Shh,' she whispered, relaxing against him. 'No questions. You're holding me.'

'And now I kiss you?'

'Tick,' she murmured.

'Close your eyes.'

She obeyed and he kissed each lid with a butterfly touch of his mouth. She waited, breath held, but when she finally opened her eyes, he was just looking at her. And so she kissed him. A brush of her lips against his.

That was all it was meant to be, but the touch of his day-old beard against her cheek stirred a darker need that shivered through them both and, with a groan, he gathered her, holding her so that his body was touching hers, warm, hard, as the kiss deepened into something fierce, desperate.

The need to breathe drove them apart but they clung together for what seemed like an age. Until Elle wished she'd told him to lie down first so that she could have held him, watched him while he slept. So that she could have been the first thing he saw when he woke.

Instead, she lifted her head. 'Lie down, Sean. Sleep for as long as you need.'

'Elle…'

'Mmm?'

'Remind me, next time I list my heart's desires, to be a little more ambitious.'

'The bathroom's through there,' she said, but she was smiling.

* * *

Sean slowly surfaced from a dream so vivid that he could still smell the scent of Elle's shampoo. Opened his eyes and for a moment had no idea where he was. He rolled onto his back. Somewhere a door banged. A dog barked and Geli's voice protested unintelligibly from somewhere below him.

Not a dream, then.

He was lying in Elle's bed, the scent was in her pillow, her sheets. He had been honest with her and she had responded. No games, no nonsense. And, clearly, if his body had berated his lack of ambition, his brain had known his limits.

Holding her, kissing her, had been beyond special, but the moment his head had hit the pillow he'd been asleep. And maybe his heart had known something else. Elle was right. They barely knew one another; they needed time to build something that would last.

It was a new concept for him, but one which, as he'd driven through the dawn, had drawn him to Elle rather than the estate, lending wings to his wheels.

He checked the time. Just gone three. Not ten hours, but long enough. Long enough without Elle beside him. He rolled off the bed and saw that she'd left him a message:

'Rocky Road, Sasparilla and Ginger Beer.'

He laughed. 'We'll get you, Rumpelstiltskin,' he said, then looked out across the garden. He was right above the lilac tree, he discovered, and tied to it there was a dog, a scruffy terrier with a battered ear, drinking from a bowl.

Geli, tearful, was looking at someone out of sight. 'There was no room at the rescue centre. I'll find her a home. I *will*!'

'Better do it before Elle gets home.' That was Sorrel. The practical one. 'She can't take on any more right now, Geli.'

He leaned out of the window. Since his car was parked in the drive, his presence could hardly be a secret.

'Is she house-trained?' Geli looked up, startled, her eyes wide to see him emerging from her sister's bedroom window. Okaaay, so he'd got that one wrong. 'The dog.'

'Absolutely!' Well, she would say that. 'It's just that her owner died and there was no one to take her in.'

'So no one would worry if I took her home with me?' he said.

'Would you?'

'I might. For a cup of tea.'

'Well... I'm *supposed* to do a home check first, to make sure you've got enough room for her. And proper fences,' she said.

'Will the Haughton Manor estate do?'

She blinked. 'All of it?'

'She'd have a couple of acres to herself, give or take the odd fox passing through.'

She shrugged. 'I suppose that would be okay, but who'll look after her during the day? When you're at work. I'm assuming you don't have a wife or a live-in partner?' she added pointedly.

'You assume right. And I'll take her with me to the office.'

'They'd let you do that?'

'I'm the boss.'

'Oh.'

He thought she'd be pleased, but instead she looked disappointed, as if she was hoping that there really was no one to take the dog. So that she could keep her.

'Of course I will need someone to take care of her in the evenings when I help Elle with Rosie. Or if I have to go away for a day or two.'

'It would have to be someone responsible,' Geli said.

'Absolutely, and I'm prepared to pay the top rate for a reliable dog-sitter. If you can recommend anyone, Angelica?'

'Well, I suppose you could bring her here,' she said casually. 'I could look after her. Elle couldn't object to that, since she wouldn't be costing us anything.'

'On the contrary,' he said. 'So? Will I do?'

He heard himself making a commitment. Open-ended. He should be panicking but he wasn't.

'I'll give you a trial period of a month. Just to make sure you take to one another.' She sighed. 'And if you're going to sleep here on a regular basis, you'd better call me Geli.'

Sorrel stepped into view, looked up. She didn't say anything. Just smiled and raised both thumbs in approval behind her sister's back.

'Where is Elle?' he asked when he joined them in the garden, folded himself up to make the acquaintance of his new best friend. She practically threw herself at him.

'She left a note to say she'd gone to fetch Gran.' Geli lifted her shoulders in an awkward little shrug. 'She wanders off sometimes, gets on a bus, then phones Elle in a panic when she doesn't know where she is.'

'I'll go and fetch them,' he said, taking out his phone, digging in his pocket for his car keys. And coming up empty-handed. Which explained why Geli hadn't seen his car. Elle had taken his vintage Jaguar coupé on a granny hunt…

In his ear, Elle's phone went to voicemail, which probably meant that she was still behind the wheel. Hopefully on her way home.

'Lovage…' he went inside '…thanks for the respite care. I hope Lally's okay. Give me a call if I can do anything. You'll find my fuel charge card in the glove compartment if you need it,' he added, giving her the pin number. Something else he'd never done. 'I'm going home now to change into something that doesn't sparkle but I'll be back later for a slice of that cake.' Then he called for a taxi.

'Can I get you some toast or something?' Geli asked when he rejoined them in the garden, clearly eager to show her gratitude.

'Thanks,' he said, 'but right now…' He looked at the dog. 'What's her name?'

'Mabel.'

'Mabel. Right… Well, Mabel and I have to go shopping for dog stuff. Food. Bowls. A basket.' The dog, he discovered, was listening. Following his every move with desperate, anxious eyes.

He took a breath, said, 'Tell your sister that I'll pick up some pizza.' If she'd been out all day hunting her grandmother, the last thing she needed to do was cook.

'No worries. I'm making a spag bol.' Sorrel smiled at him. 'You could pick up some Parmesan cheese, if you like.'

His car was pulled up neatly in the drive when he returned bearing a block of Parmesan soon after six. He resisted the twitchy need to check its immaculate bodywork and instead walked through the rear, Mabel hard on his heels.

There was no one in the kitchen. 'Hello?'

He put the cheese on the table, peered into the morning room. Lally, dozing in front of the television, opened her eyes.

'Where's Elle?' he asked.

'Oh…er…I think she went upstairs…'

Elle lay back amongst the crumpled sheets, exhausted from driving on pins in Sean's beautiful car. From tension. She was always afraid of what she'd find when her grandmother wandered but she'd been sitting in a pub being chatted up by some old guy who'd bought her a drink.

This was perfect. The pillow smelled of Sean and she nestled her cheek where his had been, breathing in the spicy scent of his shampoo, or his aftershave, listening to her messages. Sorrel asking if she was okay. Her phone company trying to sell her a more up to date package. Sean… Oh, help! Oh, bless…

She hit call back, waited impatiently. Somewhere in the house a phone began to ring and she sighed, recognising the ring of Rosie's BlackBerry.

Geli was out. Sorrel had gone to the village shop to fetch cream to fill the cake.

No… It had stopped now. Sorrel must be back.

Sean answered his phone. 'Elle?'

'Sean…'

'You sound surprised. You did call me?'

'Sorry, I just...' She stopped. 'Yes. I called you. I've just got home and picked up your message. I'm sorry about taking your car.'

'It's okay. I'm glad it was there for you. All well?'

'Yes. Gran decided to go off and look for Basil. She caught the bus to Melchester, but got off when she recognised a pub they all used to go to. It was all changed inside and when he wasn't there she panicked.'

'Have you asked her what RSG means?'

'On the way home. No joy.'

'Just a thought. What are you doing?' he asked.

'Right now?'

'Right now.'

'I'm lying with my head in the dent you made in my pillow.'

'I wish I was still there,' he murmured.

'Me too.' Wished he was lying beside her instead of just being a disembodied voice in her ear. 'I wish you were here, lying beside me, holding me. Kissing me.'

'You'll have to move over,' he said.

'Get here and I will,' she said, then, as there was a tap on her door, she realised that the sound in her ear was the dialling tone.

'Come in...'

The door swung open.

'Sean...'

'Your wish is my command.'

She didn't speak, just moved over and he came and sat beside her, kicked off one of his shoes.

'Sean! Mabel has just eaten half a pound of Parmesan cheese!' Sorrel called up the stairs.

'Mabel?' Elle queried.

'A dog.' He pushed his foot back into the shoe, took her hand, pulled her to her feet, held her for a moment. Kissed her. 'It's a long story. Maybe we should go for a walk while I tell you. I suspect, right now, she's a walking time bomb.'

'Where on earth did she come from?' Elle asked as they headed across the Common towards the riverbank. 'If I'd imagined you with a dog it would have been some glossy pedigree, not that sorry excuse for a mutt.'

'Her owner died. She had nowhere to go.'

'So you took her in?' The commitment-phobic male who didn't have as much as a goldfish in his spare and beautifully furnished home? Why wasn't she buying that? 'Between waking up this afternoon and now?'

'It was an emergency.'

'So would that be permanently? Or until you can find a good home for her?' she asked.

'A dog isn't just for Christmas, Elle.'

'A pity more people didn't realise that. I suppose you could change her name,' she said.

'Wouldn't that confuse her?'

'Actually, I don't think dogs care what you call them. As long as you call them.'

'And what about you? Are you Elle this evening? Or Lovage?' he said.

'Is there a difference?' she asked carelessly. As if she didn't know.

'There is a touch of split personality about you. This morning you were most definitely Lovage. Warm, loving, with passion simmering just beneath the surface. You were Lovage when I arrived just now, but you seem to have morphed into the practical, down-to-earth Elle.'

'Is that a problem?'

'No. I like you both,' he said.

They walked beside the river, with Mabel eagerly sniffing every tree. Called at the pub for a drink. Had something to eat sitting outside. Were home by nine.

Sean shut Mabel in the Land Rover, then walked Elle as far

as the side gate. 'What have we got this week with Rosie?' he asked.

'We?'

'I feel bad about abandoning you to Rosie's moods yesterday.'

'I coped. I will cope. It's my business, Sean, and I'm taking it seriously.'

'Does that mean you'll be giving in your notice at the Blue Boar?' he asked casually.

'Not yet. Not until I know Rosie is capable of supporting us. I need to know that I have some money coming in.'

'Scared?'

'Witless. So thank you. I would be grateful for your help at the company reception on Wednesday,' she said.

'That would be a black lace dress affair?'

'Absolutely.'

'Then nothing will keep me away. Anything else?'

Oh, yes. What she wanted, had wanted all evening with a scratchy kind of longing, was for him to kiss her witless. Be the man she'd left in her bed that morning. But he was right. She was being practical, careful Elle and he was taking his cue from her. Being a friend.

'Don't worry about Wednesday. You're a busy man and Sorrel is going to help me,' she assured him.

He put a hand against the wall behind her, leaning in, backing her up so that she could feel the warm brick catching at her hair, pulling it free from the restraining plait. 'That would be the Sorrel who's been working all week to get *Scoop!* up and running. The same Sorrel who isn't supposed to be deflected by anything until she's got a first class degree?'

She could feel his breath against her temple. Her own breath seemed stuck somewhere between in and out and going nowhere.

A hot, sexy friend who was turning her insides to mush and tossing sense out of the window.

'Good point,' she gasped. 'But if you take her place, who'll look after Mabel?'

Elle being practical. Showing him how commitment worked.

'Geli said she'd dog-sit any time.'

'Geli? When?' Then, catching on, 'Is this one of her waifs and strays?'

'Not now. I'm on a month's trial, but I'm not giving her back.'

'Wednesday, then. Six o'clock.'

'I'll be here.'

She swallowed. 'Great. Can Mabel wait while you have a cup of…tea?'

Sean smiled at the way she'd carefully avoided the 'coffee' euphemism.

'I'm sorry.'

Truly sorry. He'd had time to think this afternoon. About Elle. About himself. About the two of them. He didn't want this to be some casual relationship that they fell into and then out of as quickly. He wanted to get to know her. Wanted her to get to know him. It was too important to rush, but right now this slow courting was scrambling his brain.

He loved the fact that they had talked this evening, shared the small stuff, laughed a lot. But it was a good thing that it was Elle in residence tonight because otherwise he wouldn't have been responsible for his actions.

'I'm afraid Mabel is not quite as house-trained as I was led to believe. She'll chew the seat to shreds if I leave her in the car. You might get Sorrel to run the Trades Descriptions Act by Geli.'

'What can I say?'

'Kiss me?' he suggested.

She swallowed. 'Kiss me,' she whispered.

And he cradled Elle's head in his hands and kissed her. A

long, lingering kiss that left him wanting more. Hopefully left her wanting more too. And then he walked away while he still could.

Mabel chewed Sean's boots, chased the ducks, stole his breakfast while he had his back turned and rolled in anything disgusting that she could find.

But then she lay on his feet beneath his desk in the office, sneaked onto the sofa at night and pressed against him to have her ears rubbed, woke him with a wet nose under his chin. And she was quick. She'd learned that while he'd tolerate the loss of his breakfast and was prepared to hose her down no matter how bad she smelled, the ducks were off limits.

And he learned, too. Learned that, like the land, people responded more readily to warmth than prickly reserve. Olivia was relaxed and was coming up with ideas for the stable block that had him eating his words. And she and Hattie were ganging up to promote the Orangery as a wedding venue. He should have hated it, but found himself enjoying the tussle. And Elle had been part of that, punting for wedding business for Rosie when they'd all had supper together at the barn with Henry and the children, down for the long weekend, after the Steam Fair.

And he'd retrieved the box that contained his mother's possessions, found a photograph of his mother.

'Your father took this,' Elle said, when he showed it to her.

'How do you know that?'

'Look at her eyes. They're shining. Anyone can see that she's looking at the man she loves. She was lovely.'

'Yes, she was. I hadn't realised.'

'Put it in a frame. Remember her, Sean.'

Elle loved having Sean at her side at evening functions. Excluding the hen night. Those girls might be wearing angel wings but when they were out for fun any man was game and she was beginning to think of him as hers.

It was dangerous, risking-the-heart territory, but that was what a heart was for. To give. And she'd already given hers. It was his. All he had to do was take it.

Sean... Well, he seemed to feel that he needed to prove something to her. Or maybe to himself. That he wasn't like her father. Or his.

That he didn't just want one thing. That he was fine with her family. Maybe getting that way with his own. Healing...

No problem. Some things were worth waiting for. Meanwhile, she had him for walks, for supper occasionally, and for kisses that made it increasingly hard to say goodnight.

And she still had the 'call me' option. His birthday, as she'd discovered from Olivia, wasn't that far off.

Sean felt his heart expand under Elle's warmth. She filled his evenings with fun, his heart with love. Shared quiet days with him with only Mabel at their heels while they explored the river, lay in the meadow, hidden from the world as the wild flowers reached full height. While he tested a strength, a certainty growing in him that he was more than he believed. While she learned to trust that he would be there for her. Always.

CHAPTER THIRTEEN

The most blissful words in any language. Vanilla ice cream with hot fudge sauce.

—Rosie's Diary

'I'M REALLY sorry, Freddy, but I can't work tomorrow. In fact, I need to talk to you about my hours.'

She'd switched shifts with the girl who owed her from the previous week but Freddy had found out and had called her in early, apparently furious. As if it made any difference to him as long as he had staff cover.

'Saturday is a big day and you are my top waitress but clearly you have more interesting things to do these days,' he said, tossing the *Country Chronicle* on his desk, open at the article featuring the television shoot in Upper Haughton. 'You appear to be running your own business around mine.'

She hadn't seen the new edition of the magazine but, as there was a large photograph of her standing in front of Rosie, describing her as 'local events entrepreneur, Elle Amery' there was no point in denying it.

'This was on the sixth?' he said. 'The same day as the "family crisis" that kept you from work?'

'It was a family crisis. My great-uncle has disappeared and I had to stand in for him. He'd signed a contract with the film company and they were going to sue if someone didn't turn up.'

Freddy didn't look impressed. Well, she wasn't sure she'd have believed her, either. ...*I had to spend the morning filming a television programme; I didn't want to do it, honest, but I didn't have any choice...* Not the world's most convincing excuse.

'I suppose this is why you've been swapping your shifts, letting other women take them when you're too busy for the day job? Did you think I wouldn't notice?'

'I never left you without cover,' she said, wondering why on earth she was feeling so guilty. It wasn't as if he'd paid her for the day she'd missed. 'It's why I can't work on Saturday. Rosie, that's the ice cream van,' she explained, 'is booked for a wedding.'

'I see. And yet I seem to remember that not long ago you were asking me for extra hours because of yet another financial crisis at Chez Amery.'

'It was all very sudden, Freddy—'

'And then, of course, there's the small matter of the dress you ruined.'

'Excuse me?'

'The Honourable Miss Pickering, the young lady whose dress you drenched while you were flirting with her boyfriend, brought in the receipt. She expects compensation.'

'A few drops of water wouldn't ruin a linen dress,' she protested.

'She said it was wild silk.'

'Not in a million years. She's trying it on.'

Freddy reached out, touched her cheek with the tips of his fingers. 'No, my dear. I think that would be you.'

She took a step back. 'Me?'

'Little innocent, Elle Amery. Leading me on with those big eyes. Promising me. Soon, soon... But always making me wait a little longer. All lies.'

'Freddy,' she said sharply, hoping to make him snap out of it, get a grip. She backed away, stumbling against a chair. He was on her before she could move, trapped against the edge of his desk, the wall to one side, Freddy the other.

'I've been good to you, Elle. So good to you. And so patient.' She tried not to flinch as he stroked her jaw, but almost fainted as his thumb brushed over her lips. He caught her with his other hand, his fingers biting into her arm as he held her up, pushing her back against the desk with his body. 'Very good and very patient and it's time to stop playing the innocent little girl with me.'

'Freddy...' This time the word was squeezed through her throat as he leaned closer.

'But you're not a little girl any more, are you?'

Oh, no. No, no, no...The words were filling her head but they couldn't make it through the fear blocking her throat, a great hard lump...

'I saw the way you looked at that man. He left a note and his telephone number, but I won't have you picking up men right under my nose.'

This was her fault.

Freddy had always been protective of her. She'd been so young when she'd started working for him and he knew her history, the trouble she and her family were in. She'd been grateful for his help, even though she'd always known, on some subconscious level, that it was more than a fatherly interest. That she needed to take care.

But the job had been too important and she'd ignored the warning voices, pushing them to the back of her mind. And everything had been fine, under control. Until this moment, she had never felt threatened by him.

'I've seen you with him. Walking across the Common when you should have been here, with me...'

Noooo...

If she didn't do something, scream, use her knee, fight him, he was going to touch her, kiss her. Do something much worse.

Cleaners. Where were the cleaners?

But it was as if her vocal cords were set in concrete and, like a rabbit caught in the headlights of a car, nothing was getting through from her brain to her limbs.

His breath was on her cheek, his mouth inches from her own and the further back she leaned to escape him the more vulnerable she became.

She was close to blacking out, gasping for breath, when a sharp rap on the door had Freddy spinning round, leaving her slumped against the wall, struggling for breath.

'Who let you in?' Freddy gasped. 'We're not open.'

'A cleaner was just leaving but I'm not here to eat.' Sean stepped from the shadow of the lobby and into the office, his face set in the expressionless mask that she'd seen once before.

'I'm sorry to disturb you at work, Elle, but when I went to the house your grandmother told me that Mr Frederickson had called and asked you to come in early.'

'This is a private staff meeting—'

'I can see exactly what this is...' Sean's voice was so cold that Elle shivered '...but your quickie over the desk is going to have to wait until I've passed on a message.'

What? Then, bypassing the 'quickie' remark, 'What message? Have you found Basil? Where? Where is he?' It came out as little more than a croak.

He didn't answer, simply handed her a postcard with a picture of Brighton Pavilion on one side. On the other was a brief message:

Thought I was a goner, but it turned out to be a gallstone. Spending a few days by the sea. Keep an eye on Rosie for Lovage. I'll be home at the weekend. Basil.

'He's okay,' she said.

'Apparently. RSG *is* the Royal St George. But it's a hospital.'

Sean turned away from her flushed cheeks, tousled hair, the

unfastened top button on her shirt, calling himself every kind
of fool.

He'd seen it on that Saturday night, when Freddy had pawed
her and she'd smiled right back at him.

He'd seen the way she'd blushed when Sorrel had teased her
about the man, changed the subject when Geli had been rather
more forthright. The way she'd brushed aside his warning that
Freddy's interest was more than fatherly.

Idiot that he was, it had never occurred to him that she would
go to such lengths to keep her job. Keep her family. Even when
she'd told him that she would do anything for them.

Damn Basil. Damn Rosie. Damn his own foolishness for
falling for the blushing innocence. No one that innocent could
have played him so sweetly, drawing him in despite his determination to run, not walk away. Left him weak with frustrated
longing with phone teasing innuendo.

That she was her mother's daughter there could be no doubt.
While he'd been daydreaming about days on the river, walking
her through the wild flower meadow that he'd regenerated, his
head in the clouds, she'd have had him over Rosie's counter that
first Sunday if her sisters hadn't come home unexpectedly.

He didn't have a problem with that. She was free to do what
she wanted, with whom she wanted. It was her dishonesty that
curdled in his gullet.

At least with Charlotte there had been no pretence.

But Elle had made him believe in the possibility of forever,
made him want it. Him. Sean McElroy. The man who'd seen
it all and had known it was all hogwash, pie in the sky, a cloud
cuckoo land fantasy from the day he was born. Who always
kept relationships casual, never got emotionally involved. Who
wasn't going to mess up his life grabbing for something as
ephemeral as love, fall into the trap of caring enough to get
hurt. Fall in love.

That he couldn't forgive.

But it finally explained why she was adamant that Sorrel
should not take a job at the Blue Boar. Elle was the sacrifice,

although not much of one if the way she'd been panting for it was any indication.

He stopped, turned.

Stupid, foolish girl. Why hadn't she gone to someone, asked for help?

Elle watched Sean walk away. He was going to leave her? He really believed she'd been a willing participant?

While fear had paralysed her, anger sent a shot of adrenaline surging through her and as Freddy made another grab for her she handed him off, jamming the heel of her hand beneath his nose then walked away.

Sean, far enough away to confirm that he'd been about to walk away and leave her, had apparently changed his mind and was coming back. Too late. She walked past him without a word.

'Elle...'

She didn't look round, didn't stop.

Behind her, the door of the Blue Boar was flung open. 'If you go now, Elle,' Freddy called after her, 'you won't have a job to come back to.'

'Constructive dismissal. Sexual harassment. Assault. You'll be hearing from my solicitor,' she said, not bothering to turn around, not missing a stride, the adrenaline still pumping hard. She'd been listening when her sister had been talking about employment law.

About to add that the Honourable Miss Pickering could go whistle for her dress, she didn't bother. Freddy had been lying about that. She'd known it the minute he'd said the dress was silk.

Behind her, she heard a car door close, the throaty purr of its engine and Sean pulled alongside her in the Jaguar she'd once borrowed with such a light heart.

'Get in, Elle,' he said, leaning across, pushing the passenger door open.

One glance confirmed that he looked as grim as she felt but

she didn't slow down from the headlong charge that was taking her home. She had to keep moving. The minute she stopped, the adrenaline would run out and she'd collapse in a shivering heap. She simply told him, in the fewest syllables possible, to leave her alone.

He cruised along the kerb, keeping pace with her. 'At least let me take you home.'

'You left me.' She kept walking. While her legs kept moving she was in control. 'I can't believe you thought I was lying back and taking one just to keep my job.' He didn't deny it. 'Well, I did tell you I'd do anything for my family. I guess you believed me.'

'If you'd seen it from where I was standing…'

'I am *not* my mother,' she declared. 'I am not *your* mother either!'

Realising that she was attracting attention from the bus queue, she crossed the road and walked across the Common. Sean abandoned his car and came after her.

'Shall I take you to the police?' he asked.

'And say what? It's his word against mine. He'll say I was willing and you'd back him up, wouldn't you?' she snarled.

She took out her phone as she walked, leaving messages for both Sorrel and Geli on their voicemail not to go near the Blue Boar on any account.

Sean kept pace with her but did not speak again, made no attempt to touch her, hold her, comfort her. He simply walked with her until she reached her gate and then watched her go inside.

Elle went straight upstairs, stood under the shower, letting the water mingle with the stupid tears that were stupidly pouring down her stupid cheeks. All tears did was make your eyes red. It was only when the water ran cold and she began to shiver that she made an effort to pull herself together, try an old trick her mother had taught her. Look for something positive in everything bad.

Freddy's attack had shaken her. It had been vile. But it had forced her to face up to something that deep down she knew, had been doing her best to ignore as she clung to her safety net.

Sean... Well, he had, whether he believed it or not, rescued her. And he had warned her about Freddy. Which made her a fool if nothing worse, she acknowledged as she plugged in the hairdryer. He'd also brought her good news of Basil who'd apparently been afraid he was dying and was now living it up in Brighton.

She picked up the postcard that she'd been clutching as she walked home. Winced. Realised that her hand was swollen. Just how hard had she hit Freddy?

No. She refused to waste another second of her life thinking about him. From now on she would devote herself to making *Scoop!* a success.

Not just something to fit in around the 'day' job but something to build on, make her own. Her dream. And as she dried her hair she crowded out the horror of what had just happened by making lists in her head of the stuff she still had to do.

That was scary too but, the minute she stopped, Sean McElroy filled the vacuum. His blue eyes. The way his hair fell across his forehead, his jeans clung to his backside. His expressionless face as he'd stood in the doorway of Freddy's office seeing yet another woman who had no moral core.

Sean, who had no concept of permanency in relationships. Who assumed the worst because he never looked for the best.

She wanted to weep again. Not for herself, or for the possibility of something special that they'd lost, but for his impoverished life.

She sighed. Time to put the bad stuff behind her, go and find Gran and tell her that Basil was okay. That he'd be home soon. Home. Not some rented cottage on the Haughton Manor estate, but here, where he belonged.

Looking on the bright side, she now had all the time in the world to get stuff ready for the wedding.

She folded up the Blue Boar's black uniform, not sure what to do with it—returning it was not an option—and pulled on a pair of the brightest shorts she could find, with a tank top, and went, barefoot, into the kitchen.

The pink kettle was still hot and she found her grandmother, straw gardening hat tilted at a saucy angle, in the morning room, enjoying a cup of tea.

She wasn't alone.

'Oh, there you are, Elle,' her grandmother said. 'Sean tells me that he's heard from Basil.'

'Yes. He sent a postcard.'

'Really? Where from?'

'Brighton,' she said shortly, picking up the teapot. Sean rescued it before she dropped it and poured tea into a waiting cup.

'You're harder to get rid of than a bad penny,' she said ungratefully.

'You're not the first person to say that. Let me see your hand,' he said calmly.

'It's nothing,' she said, not wanting him to touch her, but, as she jerked away, she knocked it on the table, cried out. 'Owww... That hurt.'

'Not as much as Freddy's broken nose, if that helps,' he said wryly.

'No...' Okay, she'd hit him and maybe there had been a bit of a crunch, but... She shook her head. 'No.'

'You didn't see the blood. Come on, let's get some ice on this.' Sean kept hold of her wrist as he walked through to the kitchen, then rummaged around in the freezer until he found a tray of ice cubes. 'Rolling pin?'

Her hand was throbbing now and she didn't argue. 'First drawer.'

He tipped the ice on a tea towel and battered it until it was crushed, then, supporting her hand from beneath, he pressed the ice pack against the swelling.

'I can hold it,' she said dully, focusing on his neatly knotted tie, the perfectly ironed shirt. Not his usual working clothes. He'd been going somewhere, she thought, and had stopped by to give her the good news. Then, when he didn't let her go, 'If I broke Freddy's nose, he'll be the one coming after me for assault,'

'Nonsense. He'll tell everyone he tripped over the step.'

'He won't let me off that easily.'

'He'd be wise to consider it, or it might become a reality.'

'Don't! Please,' she said tightly.

'You're protecting him?' he bit out.

'No.' She shook her head, then forced herself to look up. Be bold, honest, true. 'I'm protecting *you*.'

His head went back as if she'd slapped him, knocked the breath out of him and for a moment neither of them spoke.

'Don't you have an estate to run?' she asked him.

He nodded, clearly relieved to be offered an escape. 'I should have been in Melchester an hour ago.'

'Then go.' Still he hesitated. 'I'll be fine.'

'You have my number…' He stopped as if realising that the offer to ride to her rescue was a hollow thing. 'I'll see you tomorrow.'

'There's no need, Sean. Sorrel and I can manage the wedding.'

'You won't be able to load up, or drive Rosie with that hand,' he pointed out. 'What time are you leaving?'

'Twelve. I have to pick up the freezer stuff from the cash and carry.'

Sean made it to the gate before the pain hit him, brought him to a halt. The realisation of what he'd lost. No, what he'd thrown away.

What kind of man was he?

He could empathise with a dead duckling suffocating in a plastic bag, but people… His mother, his ever increasing family. To them he was judgemental, harsh, cold as January charity.

All the while he'd been congratulating himself that he'd

opened up to his family, made big strides in being a man who Elle could trust, rely on, he'd been fooling himself.

When it mattered, when he'd seen Elle locked in Frederickson's arms, even though he knew her, knew what kind of woman she was, he'd instantly leapt to the wrong conclusion. Seeing only what he'd expected to see.

'Love them, keep them safe. Whatever they do.'

Her words mocked him.

He'd moved nowhere. He was still thinking of himself, of how *he* was being hurt. And yet, even when he'd let her down in the worst way, Elle was still more concerned for him than herself. Concerned that, in an attempt to redeem himself, he would be the one charged with assault.

'I'm protecting you...'

Three little words shattering the barrier layered on over the years with each loss. A barrier against feeling anything. It came at him now like a whirlwind being sucked into a vacuum. Battering him, tearing at him, cutting him.

'You have my number...'

Hollow words indeed.

He took a deep breath and began to walk back across the village to where he'd left his car. Time to put that right.

Elle tried to work, concentrate on *Scoop!* Updated *Rosie's Diary*, picking at the keys one-handed, trying not to let herself think.

She'd been forced to tell her sisters and her grandmother what had happened with Freddy, so that they understood they had to stay away from the pub. In case the police did turn up to question her. She told them as little as possible about Sean's part in the events, but he'd walked her home, told her grandmother that there had been a bit of a unpleasantness. They knew he'd been there, had drawn their own conclusions.

She knew she should contact the police herself. Make a complaint, if only to protect some other girl. Except Freddy wasn't like that with anyone else. Not even the sixth-form girls who worked at the weekend.

It was just her. Looking back, analysing it, it was all there. The obsession. She was his little virgin. His... But then Sean had turned up and suddenly she'd been snatched away from him. Spoiled...

Just thinking about it made her feel sick. Talk about sticking your head in the sand.

Sean arrived dead on time the following morning, wearing his *Scoop!* T-shirt, looking good enough to eat. The slightly haggard look just made him appear all the more dangerous.

He knocked on the back door and, unlike Mabel, who rushed in, he waited politely on the step.

'Here he is,' Geli cried as Mabel ran around her feet, hoovering up the crumbs she'd made getting herself some lunch. 'The hero of the hour.'

'What? No...'

Geli took one look at them, said, 'Walkies!' and, grabbing a sandwich, raced after Mabel.

'Some hero,' Sean said bitterly. 'What did you tell them?'

'As little as possible. Shall we go?'

This was as bad as she'd thought it would be. Worse. If there had been anyone else available to help her, she'd have called to tell him that she didn't need him. Should have called him anyway. But her hand was stiff and the pain went right up to her shoulder; also, she hadn't been able to quite give up on the hope that somehow, when she saw him, it would be all right.

Wrong.

In those few minutes when he'd thought she was Freddy's willing victim, when she had seen just how fragile a relationship could be, something had broken inside her.

Trust. There had to be trust. But she'd leapt to the wrong conclusion when she'd seen him following Charlotte from the Pink Ribbon Club Garden Party. How could she blame him for disbelieving the evidence of his own eyes?

'How's your hand?' he asked as she reached up to take Rosie's key from the hook.

'Fine.' She flexed it without thinking, then wished she hadn't. 'Thanks to your first aid.'

He beat her to the key, took her hand and looked for himself. The swelling had gone down, but there was a painful black bruise where a blood vessel had broken.

He covered it with his own hand. 'I'm sorry, Elle. I should have been the one with the sore knuckles.'

The hand covering her own bore no sign of damage and she reached for the other to reassure herself. 'So what *did* you do to him?' she asked. 'Freddy.'

'Do?'

'You must have done something. His receptionist brought me a large cheque and an apology less than an hour after you left.'

'Maybe he realised just how much trouble he was in,' he said.

'Maybe he had some help,' she said knowingly.

He shrugged. 'I just had a little chat with him. Laid out his options. Reminded him just how bad a sexual harassment case would be for business. Brought up some of the finer points of employment law.'

'But…'

'I employ seventy-odd people, Elle. I do know what I'm talking about.'

'That's it? Only Jenny, the receptionist who brought the cheque, said he'd been taken to the local A&E.'

And she'd lain awake all night imagining Sean under lock and key.

'All I did was talk to him, Elle. He blustered for a bit, but he soon saw reason, wrote a cheque to cover the salary you were owed and the compensation that would have been awarded by an employment tribunal for constructive dismissal. He wrote the apology I dictated, leaving no one in any doubt what he was apologising for.'

'That must have been more painful than his nose,' she remarked.

'You didn't see it.'

'And you don't know Freddy,' she declared, then blushed.

He laid a palm against her hot cheek. 'Neither did you.' Then, 'Once he'd despatched his receptionist, I ran him down to A&E to be patched up. And what do you know? I was right. He told the nurse that he tripped over a step.'

'Sean...'

'And, just so that you don't have to avoid that end of the village, you'll be glad to know that he's left his deputy manager in charge. The Blue Boar is going on the market from today and in the meantime he'll be taking a long vacation. For his health.'

She swallowed. 'I don't know what to say.'

'Nothing. Don't say a thing...'

A shadow crossed his face and she wanted to reach up, put her arms around him, tell him not to beat himself up. Turn her face, press her lips against the cooling hand. Before she could succumb to the temptation, he let go. Just as well.

Nothing she could say or do would change the way he was feeling right now. There was only one person who could forgive Sean for the mistake he'd made. Himself.

It made her heart ache for him. Not with pain, but with love. For a man who'd made such a big journey, found his family, opened himself up to risk. The pain would come, though, because in that instant she understood that without him there would be a cold, hollow place inside her. One that she would feel all her days.

'Come on. Let's go and stock up with lollies. Make this a wedding that no one will ever forget,' she said.

Unlikely, Sean thought later. Her hand might be sore but it hadn't stopped her giving the bride everything she wanted.

She was wearing a full-skirted calf-length dress in silvery-grey and white stripes with a black velvet belt to emphasize her waist, with little white lace gloves and a tiny black hat. Crisp, gorgeous, no one would have known from her big smile what she'd gone through in the last twenty-four hours.

After the ceremony, in the little Greek temple at Melchester Castle, she'd presented the bride with an ice cream wrapped in some frilly silver thing so that it looked like a bouquet, decorated with silver sprinkles and with a white chocolate flake that had been sprayed with edible silver food paint.

The bride removed the flake, gave it to her new husband with the words, 'On our first date, Steve, you gave me your chocolate flake. Now I'm giving you mine. Life is for sharing and this is my pledge that I'm going to share all of mine with you. All the better, all the worse. All the chocolate.'

'Is that all it takes?' Sean asked as Elle rejoined him inside Rosie. 'A chocolate flake?'

As they watched, there wasn't a dry eye in the place as he broke it in half and handed one piece back to his bride before sucking the ice cream off the half he was holding.

Just as well there was a rush from the guests to get their own ices and he had his hands full or he might have shed one himself.

How could he have ever doubted her when he'd recognised that rare innocence…? No. That was wrong. Not innocence. What made her different was a lack of guile. There was no calculation in what she did. She felt; she responded. More like her child-of-nature mother than she would want to believe.

'You did an absolutely fabulous job,' he said afterwards, as they headed back to Longbourne, silver ribbons fluttering from Rosie's extremities. 'I'll tell Hattie she has to include you and Rosie in her wedding brochure.'

'I couldn't have done it without you.'

About to say *any time, anywhere*, he realised just how hollow those words would sound to her.

'You could do anything you wanted. You're a natural, Elle.'

'You pushed me, Sean. Made me go for it. I was scared witless. And angry.' She shook her head. 'I hadn't realised how angry I was. With everyone. Basil was just one more person wanting to steal my life, but you…' She touched his arm. It was the first time she'd reached out to him since he'd let her down and it went through him like an electric shock. 'You gave it back to me.' Then, as if afraid that she'd said too much, 'Let's hope Basil hasn't changed his mind about Rosie now that he doesn't think he's about to die.'

'Elle…' He pulled over, brought Rosie to a halt in a small layby in a country lane. 'I have to say something.'

She waited. 'I'm listening,' she prompted over the ticking of Rosie's engine. The sound of the generator.

'That's my problem. I don't have the words to tell you how I bad I feel. When I think what might have happened with Freddy…'

'You stopped that. I wasn't doing well there for a minute, but you gave me time—'

'Not enough.'

'You gave me time,' she repeated, 'to save myself. And you were coming back.'

'What?'

'When I came out of the Blue Boar, you'd stopped walking away. You were facing me. Coming back for me. Why?'

'Because…' He stopped. It would be so easy to lie. So easy to say that he'd realised he was wrong and was coming back to save her. But only the truth would do. Everything that was in his heart. 'I stopped because I was so angry with you.'

'With *me*?'

'Oh, yes. I wanted to tear Frederickson apart with my bare hands, but it was you I was really angry with.' Once the flood-gates were unlocked it all came pouring out of him. 'Angry with you for letting any man do that to you. For not valuing yourself. For not punching him in the eye the first time he'd come on to you.'

'That *was* the first…'

'For not punching him in the eye the first time he touched you, held onto your arm a little too long. I wanted to shake you, Elle, tell you that you were a fool. Tell you that you are worth so much more than that. I wanted to shake you because you had made me believe and suddenly it was all falling apart. Shake you and hold you so that you'd know you never had to do that again. Hold you and tell you that I love you...' And he stopped. That was it. Those were the words. 'I love you.'

'Enough to give me your flake?' she teased shakily.

'Enough to give you my life. Will you take it?' he asked simply.

Elle looked at him. How could you resist a man who'd lay himself bare like that? Mess up and admit it. Be so painfully honest that it hurt to watch. He'd come so far in the time she'd known him. He was always a big man, challenging life, making it back down. But he'd learnt to be kind to himself. Let people close enough to hurt and, when it had hurt, he'd still come back for more.

She'd fallen in lust with him at first sight. Thought she'd grown to love him. But this feeling was bigger than that. They'd been good for each other. Each challenging the other's fear and bringing out something shining and new in a few short weeks. What could they achieve in a lifetime?

'Final answer?' she asked.

'That depends. Because I'll go on asking until I get the right one.'

There was a rap on the serving hatch. 'Excuse me, but are you open? Only we'd like an ice,' a voice said.

Elle gave a little gasp and then burst out laughing.

'We really are going to have to stop meeting like this,' Sean said, hauling himself out of his seat. 'Can I get you something?'

'Yes,' she said, grinning. 'But it will wait.'

Rosie came to the wedding all gussied up in pink and white ribbons. Basil was in charge, decked out in a striped blazer and straw boater.

Geli rode the ice cream bicycle in matching gear, handing out ice lollies to visitors to the estate as well as wedding guests.

All Sean's nieces, under the control of Sorrel, gorgeous in pale mint silk, were dressed in ice cream coloured tulle.

In the Orangery Basil walked Elle through their friends and family as a harpist played 'Greensleeves', and delivered her to Sean.

The ceremony was brief but moving and afterwards the word for the reception was definitely *fun*. Hattie had created a marquee that looked like a seaside show tent, flags flying. Olivia had found a Punch and Judy man to entertain the children. And there was candyfloss, bouncy castles, roundabouts and a ride-on train. There were donkey rides, too. And even a mini beach with buckets and spades.

Sean, caught by Elle's grandmother, looked around for Elle. She seemed to have disappeared and he wanted to slip away to the barn where they were spending the night before leaving for their honeymoon in the morning.

He'd shared her with everyone for long enough.

A mobile phone began to ring and Lally pulled it out of her pocket. 'Hello? Oh, it's for you,' she said.

'Me?' He took the phone. 'Sean McElroy?'

'Remember you said when I had a free evening to call you?'

'Vividly.'

'Well, if you can find me, it's your birthday.'

He found her waiting for him in one of the Adirondack chairs overlooking the river, a cold box at her feet.

He leaned over and kissed her. 'Is that ice cream you've got in the cool box?'

'I've decided that today is your birthday, Sean,' she said, lifting her arms and sliding them around his neck. 'It's time to unwrap your present.'

He lifted her to her feet, held her. 'Since I found you, my Elle, my Lovage, I've been reborn. Every day has been a gift.' And his kiss was a promise that he would make it his life's work to return the treasure a hundredfold.

Harlequin® Romance

Coming Next Month

Available July 12, 2011

You can find more information on upcoming
Harlequin® titles, free excerpts and more at
www.HarlequinInsideRomance.com.

HRCNM0611

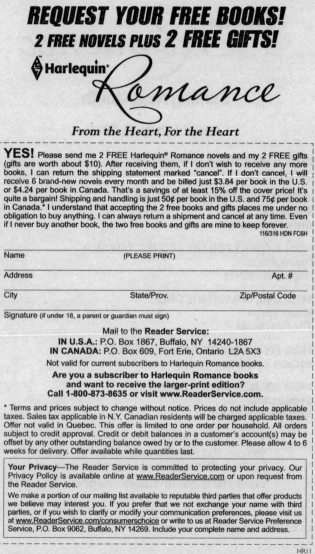

USA TODAY *bestselling author B.J. Daniels*
takes you on a trip to Whitehorse, Montana,
and the Chisholm Cattle Company.

RUSTLED

Available July 2011 from Harlequin Intrigue.

As the dust settled, Dawson got his first good look at the
rustler. A pair of big Montana sky-blue eyes glared up at
him from a face framed by blond curls.

A woman rustler?

"You have to let me go," she hollered as the roar of the
stampeding cattle died off in the distance.

"So you can finish stealing my cattle? I don't think so."
Dawson jerked the woman to her feet.

She reached for the gun strapped to her hip hidden under
her long barn jacket.

He grabbed the weapon before she could, his eyes nar-
rowing as he assessed her. "How many others are there?"
he demanded, grabbing a fistful of her jacket. "I think you'd
better start talking before I tear into you."

She tried to fight him off, but he was on to her tricks and
pinned her to the ground. He was suddenly aware of the soft
curves beneath the jean jacket she wore under her coat.

"You have to listen to me." She ground out the words
from between her gritted teeth. "You have to let me go. If
you don't they will come back for me and they will kill
you. There are too many of them for you to fight off alone.
You won't stand a chance and I don't want your blood on
my hands."

"I'm touched by your concern for me. Especially after
you just tried to pull a gun on me."

"I wasn't going to shoot you."

Dawson hauled her to her feet and walked her the rest of the way to his horse. Reaching into his saddlebag, he pulled out a length of rope.

"You can't tie me up."

He pulled her hands behind her back and began to tie her wrists together.

"If you let me go, I can keep them from coming back," she said. "You have my word." She let out an unladylike curse. "I'm just trying to save your sorry neck."

"And I'm just going after my cattle."

"Don't you mean your boss's cattle?"

"Those cattle are mine."

"*You're* a Chisholm?"

"Dawson Chisholm. And you are…?"

"Everyone calls me Jinx."

He chuckled. "I can see why."

Bronco busting, falling in love…it's all in a day's work.
Look for the rest of their story in

RUSTLED

Available July 2011 from Harlequin Intrigue
wherever books are sold.